Not True Stories from Oregon

Arran N. Gimba

iUniverse, Inc.
New York   Bloomington

Not True Stories from Oregon

This is a work of fiction. All of the characters, names, incidents, organizations, and dialogue in this novel are either the products of the author's imagination or are used fictitiously.

iUniverse books may be ordered through booksellers or by contacting:

iUniverse
1663 Liberty Drive
Bloomington, IN 47403
www.iuniverse.com
1-800-Authors (1-800-288-4677)

Because of the dynamic nature of the Internet, any Web addresses or links contained in this book may have changed since publication and may no longer be valid. The views expressed in this work are solely those of the author and do not necessarily reflect the views of the publisher, and the publisher hereby disclaims any responsibility for them.

ISBN: 978-1-4502-5798-5 (sc)
ISBN: 978-1-4502-5805-0 (dj)
ISBN: 978-1-4502-5804-3 (ebk)

Library of Congress Control Number: 2010913483

Printed in the United States of America

iUniverse rev. date: 10/29/2010

This book is dedicated to my mom, my dad, Jason, and Emily.
Love you all.

This book is not dedicated to the people for whom Oprah has said
recently is a major influencing factor in decision making; people
who borrow your jacket and then return it with Kleenex in the
pockets; people who come into a room and yell, "What are you
doing?" when it is fucking obvious what you are doing; people who
keep talking and talking to you when you feel like shit and don't
feel like talking to anyone; people who repeat themselves; people
who repeat themselves; people who don't know that they have bad
breath; people who talk to television and movie characters, as if the
characters can hear them; people who tell long, elaborate jokes that
go on forever and then fuck up the punchline; people who smoke
right outside the door of a non-smoking establishment, getting smoke
all over everybody who enters/leaves; people who clear their throats
in a disgusting way; people who send greeting cards that spill glitter,
sequins, or confetti on the hapless recipient; people who spell "you're"
as "your"; and people who are fans of the Los Angeles Lakers.
Hate you all.

contents

Acknowledgments

So we meet again (and for those who didn't read my first book, where the hell were you?) I never thought about writing a second book. I was hoping that my first book, *To Light a Fire and Other Short Stories*, would become so successful, I would just live the rest of my life on its royalties. I was hoping I could be one of those one-and-done authors like Harper Lee, who wrote *To Kill a Mockingbird*. But, nope, that didn't happen.

They say that a sequel is never as good as the first. I mean, *Caddyshack II* was horrendous at best (every guy I know can quote lines from the original, but no one would be caught dead quoting a line from that debacle). *Batman and Robin* was God-awful (when Mr. Freeze's henchmen decide to skate around in hockey gear and cause mayhem without any trace of ice, you knew you were in for a shit smeller). And *Grease 2* was, well, deplorable (Michelle Pfeiffer in a giant Christmas tree costume... 'nuff said).

I felt like I didn't have anything to lose with this book. If this book sucked, then meh, it would be just like every other sequel. But if this book rocked the house (that's what the cool kids say), then I hit the jackpot.

This time, I wanted to celebrate the great state of Oregon, the birthplace of the microbrew craze, hippies, and bikers who run though red lights wearing those God-awful bright spandex tights (seriously, why?). By the way, in Oregon, biker means cyclist. In every other American city, biker means "one who rides a motorcycle."

You probably don't know a whole lot about us Oregonians. Well, let me tell you something; we are the nicest people in the country. If we found a wallet with $500 in it, we would give it back to the owner. People help me all the time when I go shopping at Fred Meyer … and they don't even work at the damn place. Hell, if I ever got shot by a robber from Portland, the robber would say, "Oh dear, I hope I didn't kill you." We are super friendly!

We are also the home of unpredictable weather. In one day, we could see sun, rain, snow, and then more rain. We believe our weathermen, even though the chances of getting an accurate forecast from them is cloudy at best. Oh yeah, we love weather puns.

But more importantly, we are the home of weird. From art cars to zombie walks, Oregon is a fantastically unique place. These 21 stories all take place within the state. After reading them, you should gain a better understanding of just how wonderful and weird Oregon really is.

There are a lot of people who I need to thank and, without them, this second book would have never been written. First, my mom and dad for bringing me into this world. That's kind of important.

I also have to thank the following editors who made this book so awesomely awesome: Allison Itterly, Diane Pertindeau, Greg Heyman, Jayna Braden, Danna Solomon, Emily Burrows, David Simon, and, of course, my mom. Without them, my writing would have been worse than those Nigerian scam letters. I also want to thank Ashleigh Burgess for taking my photo for the back of the book.

I do not want to thank my neighbor's dog for constantly barking during my time writing this book. Dog people are the strangest people on earth. Why would you ever buy a thing that demands you walk it everyday, is infested with bugs, licks your face after licking another thing's ass, and poops everywhere? Makes absolutely no sense to me. Yes, I know, I made fun of cat people in the last book. I'm an equal-opportunity offender. I'll make sure to insult parrot people in the next one.

Finally, I would like to thank Jamba Juice for providing me with enough Orange A-Peel smoothies to make me pee orange for the next eight years. And, yes, my Dell Inspiron 9300 laptop is still alive and kicking. Sorry, Apple. Maybe next year.

LOVE is overrated

"Love doesn't make the world go round. Love is what makes the ride worthwhile."

Franklin P. Jones

Ventura Cooper adjusted his dreadlocks and tried to get people to shake his hand. He was standing on the corner of NW 23rd and Johnson, a tattooed/greasy/tight black pants hipster version of Portland's Rodeo Drive. Boutiques and fancy clothing stores lined the potholed-infested street as canvassers stood on each corner. Ventura was not an ordinary hippie canvasser. In reality, he was a living cupid.

But Ventura wasn't trying to link two people together in holy matrimony. He was the complete opposite. His job was to break couples up. When he shook the hands of the man or woman, they were destined to break up. For example, he shook the hand of Glen Hoover, a wonderful old man who'd been married for over twenty-five years. That evening, Glen decided to end his marriage over 'irreconcilable differences.'

On another day, Ventura shook the hand of a maxillofacial radiologist by the name of Angela Styron. Later that night, she cheated on her boyfriend … and she got caught. That relationship ended quite horribly. Her boyfriend threw a fit and punched the guy she'd cheated with. Angela became hysterical and slapped her boyfriend, breaking her pinky in the process. And, the poor sucker who'd only wanted a good time, ended up with two missing teeth and a hand towel to cover his private parts as he ran out of the motel room.

Ventura loved breaking hearts. It gave him a great thrill, the kind of thrill a kid gets when he shoots eggs at a car, or when a teen throws an empty bottle of beer in the air and watching it shatter on the pavement.

Ventura stood on the corner, shifting from side to side, waiting. He was good at that. And then he spotted a young man with a grunge haircut, torn jeans, holding a worn-down guitar case in one hand.

Ventura reached into his pocket and pulled out a small photo. Max Suller was his name.

Ventura moved closer then stuck out his hand. "Hi there, how are you doing today?" he asked.

Max shook his hand. "Good, good."

"Can I talk to you for a second about the Green Party?"

"I can't, sorry. I've got a concert to rehearse for."

"Okay, sir, have a nice day."

As Max walked away, Ventura smiled at the thought of another heart broken.

***

When his shift ended, Ventura headed home. As he ambled down Burnside, past the Marathon Tavern, he saw Kelli Mehling crying on the front steps of a small house. Kelli looked like one of those Suicide Girls he'd seen on the Internet—dyed pink hair and an impressive number of piercings and tattoos. On any other day, he would have walked on, barely noticing her. But today, seeing her cry affected him. It disturbed him even.

"Are you okay?" Ventura asked.

Kelli stared up at him with watery eyes, mascara streaming down her cheeks. "I'm good, thanks." She sniffled and wiped her nose on the sleeve of her shirt.

"If that's the definition of feeling good, then I don't ever want to feel good."

Kelli smiled a little. "It's my boyfriend. He's being an ass."

Ventura sat down next to her. "Like how, if I may ask?"

"It's nothing. We just got into a fight. I don't even know what we fought about. And I thought I knew him really well. We were like this." She pressed the tips of her index fingers together. "I guess I was wrong. I don't know anything about him."

A commotion came from behind them—shouting accompanied by the sound of objects being thrown around. The door flew open and Max Suller stormed out.

"Here are your damn clothes, you filthy whore!" He threw an armful of sweaters, leggings, and some provocative-looking underwear on the ground. Without even looking at Kelli, Max went back into the house and slammed the door.

Ventura swallowed a lump in his throat. *Holy shit*, he thought. Although he enjoyed his profession, he had never actually seen the repercussions of his actions. Broken hearts were just some abstract notion, something to get over, to move on from. Seeing the ache and the pain in person, seeing it up close touched Ventura in a way he'd never expected. It shook him like he had never been shaken before.

"You have a place to stay?" Ventura asked.

"Yeah, I'll stay at a friend's place for a while," Kelli whimpered.

Ventura nodded. He wanted to offer a few words of wisdom, but, truth was, he had none. Absolutely no word of encouragement or sympathy came to him. "All right. Try to have a good night. Sorry about what happened."

As Ventura ventured down the lonely streets, it started to drizzle. It seemed to always be drizzling in Portland. He felt the mist on his face, on his lips. He couldn't shake Kelli off his mind. Her puckered lips, her blue eyes, her tiny black-painted fingernails. And, the sad look on her face. He was the cause of that.

That night, Ventura tossed and turned. He couldn't sleep. The humid air hung heavy in his room. Kelli's face haunted him, and the sound of her sniffles seemed to fill his bedroom. Did girls really cry so much over some guy? He had no idea what a broken heart felt like, but it sure seemed bad. He felt awful. Why was this affecting him so much? When he saw Kelli sobbing, he felt his body go numb. He wasn't supposed to feel guilt or remorse.

Ventura flung off the covers and grabbed his cell phone. He needed some advice. He called his friend Larry, another cupid.

***

It was well past midnight when Ventura walked into the Dirty nightclub in downtown Portland. Dirty was the raunchiest nightclub in the city, and Ventura didn't understand what Larry was doing in such a place. Dance music by Rihanna blared through the speakers as girls pole danced. Well, maybe he understood the appeal a bit.

He strolled through more skin than he'd seen in his life and finally found Larry sitting at a table in the back with a beautiful blonde whose breasts were about to burst out of her white halter top. Larry lived in Gresham, a place just outside Portland where people go to escape being awesome. He spent more time in this club than home.

"Ventura, my buddy, my pal!" Larry yelled. He was eating a slice of pepperoni pizza with one hand and fingering the blonde's thigh with the other. A string of cheese clung to his chin. The blonde seemed completely enamored by his charm, despite the pepperoni-filled gut and thinning hair.

"Hey, Larry," Ventura replied. He took a seat across from the pair. He always wondered how Larry got the girls. Larry was short, stout, and balding. And, he treated women like crap. Slapping their asses, telling them to show more cleavage. It was a miracle he got any women at all. But, he was a cupid, and he knew how to work his magic. Ventura had to give him that.

Ventura didn't consider himself ugly, but he was shy around the female species. He had been told in the past that he had "stunning" green eyes, and "bodacious" dreadlocks, but because of his profession, he steered clear of women.

Well, not exactly.

The closest Ventura had ever come to a broken heart was when he met Jennifer. His heart felt funny just thinking about her. She was the barista at Starbucks in Pioneer Courthouse Square. Ventura had ordered a vente caramel Frappuccino and met her gaze. Brown eyes like a doe.

"Do you want whip cream on that?" Jennifer had asked.

Ventura stared.

"Sir, do you want whipped cream?"

"I want to take you to dinner." The words just fell out of his mouth.

Jennifer smiled, a beautiful smile, perfect straight teeth. "I'm sorry," she said, "but I have a boyfriend." Her stare lingered.

"That's okay," Ventura said. He read her nametag. "You have a great day, Jennifer."

Oh, there was something about Jennifer. Maybe it was the fact that she was unavailable, or how she continually smiled as she worked the cappuccino machine. Or how her fingers gently touched the top of Ventura's hand as she handed him his drink. Yes, there was something about Jennifer.

And Ventura felt that something with Kelli. Her crying made a part of him shake. How their eyes locked. He felt an urge to hold and comfort her, to never make her sad again.

Larry looked at the blonde and patted her thigh. "I need to talk to my friend. Can you give us some privacy?"

"Sure," the blonde giggled. "Afterwards, will you give me some privacy?"

Larry spanked the blonde's ass as she walked away. He laughed. "Isn't she great?"

"She's wonderful," Ventura replied in an "I don't give a shit" tone of voice.

"You want a Hand Solo?" Larry asked.

"A Hand Solo?"

Larry laughed. "It's a slice of pizza. That's what they call it here. Isn't it great? Isn't it dirty?"

"Whatever. Larry, I need to talk to you."

"About what?"

"I need you to put two people back together."

Larry just about spat the pizza out of his mouth. "What? Why?"

"I need you to put two people back together," Ventura repeated.

"But you're the biggest heartbreaker this side of the Willamette. Why would you want to put a couple back together? Are you kidding me, bro?"

"No," Ventura said. He rolled his eyes.

"Why the sudden change of heart?"

Ventura cleared his throat and thought about finding the right words. "For the first time, I actually saw the repercussions of my actions. God, it was awful. The woman was crying so hard, I thought she was going to dehydrate."

Larry took a sip of beer. "You really feel this bad?"

"I do, Larry."

"This is so unlike you. I'm stunned. And I don't get to say that very often. But, there you have it. I'm stunned."

"I know! I'm losing sleep over it. It's all I can think about." Kelli's face flashed before his eyes. "I saw this girl crying her heart out," Ventura reached for a slice of pizza and took a bite, "because of me."

"Then what?"

"Then her boyfriend busted through the front door mad as all hell, yelling, and throwing panties and bras that would make the girls in here blush."

"Is that so?"

"Yeah, so will you help me?"

Larry looked around. "I was supposed to get some later with that blonde chick."

"But you can do that anytime. You're a fucking cupid."

Larry laughed. "Yeah, good point. I could do any one of these ladies if I wanted to. Hell, I could do all of these ladies if I wanted … at once."

Ventura sighed. "So, will you help me out?"

Larry thought about it while he munched on a mouthful of pizza. He guzzled a few sips of beer and let out a loud belch before finally speaking. "All right, fine, I'll do it. But you have to do something for me in return."

"Anything."

"I have about thirty hotties who I've made mine. Can you help me break up from some of them?"

Ventura smiled. "Thirty women?"

"Yeah, it's been a slow month. But they all want me to marry them. Women with their damned rings… I don't want wives, I just want girlfriends. The difference between a wife and a girlfriend is about a hundred pounds. Don't ever forget that."

Ventura shook his head in disbelief. "If you give me the list of women, I can work on that for you."

Larry shook his hand. "We have a deal then, big man. Hey, can you order me some O-Gasms?"

Ventura knew the answer to his question would be stupid, but he asked anyway. "What's that?"

"Onion rings."

"Seriously? Who runs this place, a sixth grade dude?" Ventura asked.

Larry nudged him with his elbow. "Admit it. It's kinda funny."

***

Larry knocked on the door of Max Suller's house while Ventura hid behind a bush. Larry was dressed in a buttoned-down blue shirt tucked into khaki pants. Did girls really dig that look? When no one answered, Larry knocked again, louder. Finally, Max came out.

"What the hell do you want?" Max asked.

"I just wanted to say that I went to your concert and you rocked!" Larry exclaimed.

Max smiled. "Well, thank you." Larry held his hand out for a handshake. "What was your favorite song?"

Ventura frowned when he saw Larry's blank face. How was he going to lie his way out of that one?

Larry, with his hand still held out, replied, "The first one. Yeah, that first one you played was really, really good."

There was a long, agonizing pause. Ventura could practically see the gears turning in Max's head. Doubt seemed to mingle with his ego's need to believe Larry's compliment.

Would Larry's lie work?

Max smiled. An ego's need to be fed could be mighty strong sometimes. "Thanks, that's my favorite, too." He eagerly shook Larry's hand.

For a second Ventura thought Max was going to invite Larry in for a beer and a night-long discussion about music.

"You have a good night," Max said.

"You, too, bud," Larry replied. Max went inside and closed the door.

Ventura stepped out of the bush and ran up to Larry. "So, that's it?" he asked.

"He'll be madly in love with Kelli in about five minutes. But now we have to find Kelli," Larry replied. "Once I shake her hand, the two will be back together. Otherwise, we'll just have some crazy guy stalker, which wouldn't be good for her." Larry and Ventura returned to the sidewalk. "Do you know where she is?"

Ventura thought for a second. "She told me she was staying at a friend's place."

"Which friend?"

"How would I know?"

"Didn't you ask?"

"Yeah, I'm going to ask some strange girl who just broke up with her boyfriend where she's planning on staying. I'm sure she would have loved that."

Larry let out a brief sigh. "Well, tell you what, you find Kelli then call me back and I'll shake her hand."

"Will do," Ventura replied.

Larry looked at his watch. "I hope that blonde is still at Dirty. Sure would love to fuck her tonight."

"Thanks again, Larry," Ventura said.

"Not a problem. Have a good night," Larry replied as he power-walked away.

***

All week, Ventura stood at his usual post on 23rd, shaking hands, talking about those loser Democrats and Republicans and scanning the crowd for a girl with dyed pink hair.

He shook the hand of a large, heavyset woman who giggled and jiggled as he charmed her with his political banter. As soon as she stepped aside, he saw a glimmer of pink. Kelli was down the street looking through the window of an antique shop.

Ventura quickly said goodbye and raced toward Kelli. Out of breath, he stammered, "Hi, Kelli."

Kelli looked at him with a perplexed look. Then her face relaxed. "Oh … hey … how are you?" she asked.

"You remember me?"

"Yeah, I do. You made sure I was okay the other day when… well, you know."

"Yeah … how are you doing?"

"I'm feeling better. Sometimes, you just got to move on," she said.

Ventura smiled. "Exactly. Hey, quick question. I know this is going to sound really awkward, but … do you want to get some dinner tonight?" His heart pounded.

Kelli smiled and ran her fingers through her pink hair. "I would love that. Want to meet at Rose's?"

Ventura's eyes shifted across the street to Rose's, a family-owned 50's-themed diner. "Definitely. I get off my shift at six. So, how about seven?"

"Sure. Looking forward to it," Kelli replied.

"All right, see you later," Kelli said. She fiddled with her lip ring and took off down the street.

Ventura stood and watched Kelli walk away, watched until the pink got lost among the crowd. He whipped out his cell phone and called Larry.

"What do you want?" Larry said.

"I found Kelli. She'll be at Rose's tonight at seven. Can you make it?"

"Anything for you, buddy!" Larry replied.

"All right, you better be there," Ventura said.

"Relax, relax, I'll be there."

As Ventura hung up the phone he couldn't help but wonder if he was making a mistake. Maybe this was all happening for a reason. Maybe shaking Max's hand was the best thing that could have happened to Kelli. So why then, did he want Larry to shake her hand and bring the couple back together? His heart pounded, his hands shook. Maybe he should just stick to the plan.

Destiny was a funny thing.

***

The next day, Ventura was passing out leaflets encouraging people to vote Green. He insistently pressed one into the hand of a reluctant, little old woman who wanted nothing to do with green. She was set in her ways and was not about to change just so some young, entitled, over-indulged snothead could have a better world to live in.

"Who cares if the world stays green, young man?" the woman argued as she poked her finger into Ventura's belly. "All the young kids spend their time playing video games anyways. Who the hell is going to see the Amazon, or the Appalachians, or Glacier Park, or any of that shit? They just want to play—vroom, vroom, vroom, bang, bang, bang, pow, pow, pow."

Ventura shifted uncomfortably, itching to get away from the over-opinionated woman. He couldn't focus. Last night, after his shift, he blended in with the crowd and watched Kelli from a distance. She was sitting alone by the window at Rose's waiting for him. He didn't stick around to see Larry intervene.

"I'll tell you, in my day, we went outside to play..." the old woman continued.

"I'm sure you did." He looked over her shoulder and stopped dead in his tracks. Kelli was walking down the street, looking as happy as could be. She was beaming, practically skipping. Why was she so happy? He stood her up? Larry must have gone through with the plan and shook her hand. Ventura felt his stomach knot.

As the old woman continued to rattle on, Ventura tuned her out. He was hooked. He watched as Kelli moved toward him through the crowd, her lips moving to a song he couldn't hear. Oh, what he wouldn't give to be within earshot, to hear her soft voice sing a tune. He should have called the whole thing off, told Larry to forget it, that he would handle this one himself. He should have met Kelli last night.

Ventura stepped away from the old woman and headed toward Kelli. "Hey, Kelli!" he exclaimed.

"Oh, hey, Ventura," Kelli replied.

"I'm really sorry I didn't meet you for dinner last night. I couldn't get off my shift, and my boss was up my ass, and…" he rambled and lied. It didn't feel good.

"Oh, that's all right." Kelli's smile overflowed with happiness.

"You look so happy," Ventura said. "What happened?"

"I found someone special. God, he's so cute! And he's such a terrific musician."

"Glad to hear," Ventura replied. He gritted his teeth. Maybe, just maybe it was for the best.

"We're going out again tonight to see that new Julia Roberts movie."

"Well, congratulations. I'm really glad you and Max are back together."

Kelli's smile disappeared. "Max?"

Ventura was confused and wasn't sure what to say. "Yes … Max. Isn't that who you're seeing?"

"No, I've moved on from him. I'm seeing someone better."

"Who?" Ventura was afraid to hear the answer.

"This guy I met last night. His name is Larry," she replied.

Ventura's mouth opened, but he couldn't say a word.

Larry emerged from the crowd and grabbed Kelli by the waist. "Hey, Ventura!"

"Larry! What the hell?!" Ventura asked.

"She's so beautiful," Larry replied. He nuzzled his nose into Kelli's cheek.

Kelli looked at her watch. "Honey, we have to get going. We're going to be late for the movie."

"Oh, we gotta go," Larry replied.

"What instrument do you play?" Ventura challenged.

Larry smiled triumphantly. "The trombone."

"Such a harmonious sound," Kelli said as she grabbed Larry's hand.

Larry leaned in and whispered into Ventura's ear. "Thanks for bringing her to me. God, she has an awesome ass."

As Larry and Kelli walked away, Ventura stood—alone—on the corner of NW 23rd and Johnson. So this was what a broken heart felt like, with or without a handshake. He fixated on Kelli's pink hair—thought about her smile, the way she fiddled with her lip ring. There was nothing he could do as he watched her disappear around the corner.

A Lovely Dinner

"Whenever I date a guy, I think, 'Is this the man I want my children to spend their weekends with?'"

Rita Rudner

"Dead people are the best."

Those were the words spoken by Brian Harris. He whispered that message across the table to Nancy Caraway. This was, by far, the strangest date she had ever been on.

Several weeks earlier, Nancy decided to sign up for one of those online dating websites. Though she was tall and thin with blonde flowing hair and an ass to kill for, her husband, Jeff, had left her three years ago for some hot model at his agency. He accused Nancy of spending too much time working and not enough time with him, so he looked elsewhere. She thought he was the one who spent too much time working, working on boning his models. Though it was hard, She had moved on from that relationship and was content on being a workaholic.

A workaholic. Maybe she was. It depended on how you looked at it. She grew up on the East Coast in a small town right outside of Hartford, Connecticut. Her father and mother were both lawyers, and, naturally, after three years of beer pong, karaoke bars, and theme parties, Nancy decided to get more serious about college. She spent her fourth year at UCONN studying her ass off for the LSAT. She was determined to make something of her life. To make her parents proud. She was accepted into New England School of Law, not the best law school but certainly not the worst, and moved to Boston. Met Jeff. Graduated at the top of her class. Moved to Portland with Jeff. Thirty-five-years-old, separated from husband. The rest was history.

She fiddled with the napkin in her lap and watched as Brian slurped his soup from the bowl. Brian was the fourth man she'd met since signing up. The first three had been completely bizarre, to say the least. The first man was a 35-year-old psychologist named Thomas Penney. His profile looked promising—steady job, no kids. His photo, which resembled the looks of George Clooney, caught her eye and she couldn't resist. It sounded like the perfect match.

When Thomas asked her to come to his house for their date, she found him bold, but exciting. It had been awhile since she dated. Was it normal to meet at someone's house on the first date? She decided to go for it; if anything happened she had a trusty can of pepper spray. She pulled into Hillsboro, a city where all the houses looked exactly alike. The lawn was cut and flowers lined the driveway. When she knocked on the door, her heart leaped in her chest. No answer. She knocked again.

The door creaked open and a middle-aged woman with brown fluffy hair answered the door. His wife? His sister? How awkward.

"Um, I'm here for Thomas," Nancy said hesitantly.

The woman furrowed her brow. Placed her hand on her hip. "Thomas is grounded. Are you one of the teachers he shot with the paint gun?"

Nancy wanted to run. Obviously, there was no second date.

The second match was with 31-year-old Todd Hatch. He was an English professor who had a strange addiction to Sweet Tarts. That was what it said in his profile. Verbatim. *Strange addiction to Sweet Tarts! Lol – as all the students say these days!* Nancy cringed when she read that, but he seemed quirky, and she needed some excitement in her life.

The night of their date, she glanced at her watch; he was fifteen minutes late. Just as she was about to give up, he called.

"I sincerely apologize, Nancy," he said, "but my driver is running a little late. We should be there in ten minutes."

Her brain went into overdrive. She never would have imagined that an English professor would have that type of money to ride around in a limo. She made a decent chunk, and could afford a limo if need be, but she indulged in guilty pleasures – clothing, clutch bags, and shoes. A girl needed to keep up her appearance.

She rushed to her bedroom, tore off the simple little frock she'd chosen, and rummaged through her closet for something more appropriate. With her hand finally on the elegant, backless Vera Wang, she dressed faster than any woman in history. She kicked off her comfortable pumps and slipped into her new Gucci sling backs, the ones she'd not yet worn. Already out of breath, and careful not to break a sweat, she hurried to the bathroom and pinned her hair up into a sexy chignon.

Just as she slipped the last hairpin into place, she heard a car drive up. She hurried back to her bedroom, dumped the contents of her purse onto the bed, grabbed the Gucci clutch that accompanied the sling backs, and crammed as many necessities as she could into it. With a final glance at the mirror and an approving wink at her reflection, she rushed out the door.

She caught sight of the vehicle in her driveway and nearly teetered over. Breathless from her fashion race, she just stood there, gasping.

Todd emerged from the taxi, a 2001 dull gray sedan with a dent in the front fender.

"Wow! You're hot," Todd beamed.

Nancy could feel the blush of her cheeks plunge into the décolleté of her dress and all the way up to her freshly-dyed blonde roots. Her mouth opened, but nothing came out. She'd never been so speechless in her life. No words came; no thoughts. Just stunned disbelief.

Todd held the car door open for her and she entered the stinky cab, masking her disdain.

"You like fine Italian cuisine?" Todd asked as he slid in beside her.

She nodded. Maybe things wouldn't turn out that badly. He was kind of cute, though he had more hair in his profile photo. Great pasta, a fine bottle of wine, and romantic music. The night could still be salvaged.

But that fine Italian place turned out to be Pizza Hut. While Todd happily munched on breadsticks, Nancy took gulp after gulp of beer, anything to take the increasingly frazzled edge off. After they'd gone through a Venetian pizza—his idea of fine cuisine—he ordered Cinnaparts for dessert.

As he licked his fingers he said, "Um, my deal hasn't actually come through yet and I spent all my money on the taxi. Can you get this?"

She ended up paying for the pizza and the taxi home.

Her next date was with 29-year-old Anthony Jacobs. Anthony was a self-employed salesman whose profile picture was completely different from what he looked like in person. He was a little more heavy-set and his eyes had a sleepy look to them. It was clear that Anthony was very good at using Photoshop. But he really impressed her with his Armani suit and new Mercedes. He brought her to a truly elegant restaurant and this time, her Vera Wang didn't go to waste.

The bottle of wine, priced at over a hundred dollars, was excellent, as was the fine meal. Nancy could definitely get used to being treated this way.

Anthony was well spoken, though at times quite blunt. He also had a persuasive flair, something she noticed on their second date when no table was available at his favorite restaurant. A quick and private word with the maitre d' and they were quickly ushered to the best table.

On her fourth date with Anthony, he seemed a little off his game. He drove into the parking lot of Portland City Grill, but immediately turned around and left.

"I'm not really in the mood for a crowd tonight." He seemed reluctant to go out at all. "How 'bout we go to my house?" he asked.

It was their fourth date. Going to his place could be nice and she was eager to see where and how he lived. "Sure, sounds great," she replied.

Just as they were about to turn the corner that led to the Pearl District, she noticed how Anthony kept looking in his rear view mirror. He accelerated, bringing the elegant car to a speed that had Nancy gripping the door.

"Is something wrong?" she asked.

"I think a cop's following me."

She looked out her mirror to see that there wasn't just one cop car. There were three. She then heard the unmistakable sound of a helicopter and looked up; a police chopper was just overhead.

She froze. Who was this guy, and what could this mean for her career? She was a lawyer for god sakes. Getting arrested could ruin her reputation.

Anthony drove at a frantic speed, passing cars illegally, before pulling over and abandoning the car to run off. Nancy sat there stunned, unable to move, as the cops swarmed the car and arrested her. The helicopter's spotlight beamed on her. Not only was it the police chopper, but also the news helicopter had joined the chase.

As she was being cuffed, she heard the police officers scream, "Get on the ground!"

Moments later, they returned, pushing and shoving Anthony into the police car. He sneered and growled at the police, but flashed Nancy a strangely angelic smile. The police questioned her for hours, asking about her involvement or knowledge of the drugs Anthony sold. Several background checks later, she was released on bail.

Months later, Anthony called. "Hey, doll. I thought maybe you and me could hang out as soon as I get out of this joint."

The answer to that question should have been obvious to him, she thought.

After her fiasco with Anthony, she considered giving up on the whole Internet dating scene, but decided to give it one last try. She was a successful, attractive woman. Why was it so hard to find someone decent? Brian claimed to be an MD. How awful could he be?

So now here she was, sitting in a cozy little restaurant with a crazy man who'd just said he loved dead people.

"Excuse me?" Nancy asked him, drinking her wine.

"Dead people are the best," Brian reiterated. "They don't talk back, and I can do whatever I want to them."

"That's, umm, interesting." Suddenly, Nancy felt nauseous. Seconds later, she passed out. She came to and was vaguely conscious of the waiter who leaned over her. *What was in that wine?*

"Oh my goodness! I should call for an ambulance," the waiter said to Brian.

Nancy's blurred vision tried to focus on Brian's face; tried to find one ounce of concern. Instead, he seemed to be grinning. It was a strange, almost hungry smile.

"Oh no, that's not necessary," Brian replied. "She's just tired; she had a long day. I'll take her home right now."

The waiter walked away and Brian checked her pulse. She wanted to pull her wrist from his hand, but she didn't have the energy to do anything. She couldn't fight, she couldn't get up, she couldn't even speak.

Brian's smile spread over his face and brought a fanatical gleam to his eyes. He leaned in close and whispered in Nancy's ear, "Dead people are the best."

zPhone

"I just read this great science fiction story. It's about how machines take control of humans and turn them into zombie slaves! ... Hey! What time is it? My TV show is on!"

Calvin from Calvin and Hobbes

Dinah sat across from Bessie and watched her fidget with a lock of her long, black hair. Her blue eyes darted from one end of the restaurant to the other ever since she'd placed down her fork. It was their usual Tuesday lunch at Applebee's, and while they'd ordered, been served, and had eaten in a timely manner, Bessie now appeared ready to jump out of her seat.

"Where is that waitress with our check?" Bessie asked.

"Why are you in such a rush?" Dinah asked. Both were sophomores at the University of Portland, and she knew they had more than enough time to make the quick five-minute trip back in time for their next class.

"Tonight's the big night."

"This is the night you're finally going to end your virginal years?" Dinah tried to hold back on her sarcasm and wondered if Bessie noticed.

"No! The zPhone is coming out," Bessie said with a heavy dose of melodramatic excitement.

Dinah passed her fingers through her mop of curls and shook her head in disbelief.

"Why are you shaking your head like that?" Bessie asked.

"I can't believe you're going to wait in line for hours for that thing," Dinah replied.

"Have you seen the features? A multi-touch screen, a sliding keyboard, a video camera, GPS navigation, Internet access, nail clipper..."

"Who cares?" Dinah interrupted. "It's just a stupid phone. A stupid, overpriced phone."

"It's not just a stupid phone. It's the hottest thing in the world. I even saw pictures of Silvia Sweetheart carrying one around." She paused. Her eyes widened. "My God, Silvia Sweetheart has one!"

"So if Brad Pitt jumped off a cliff, would you do it too?" Dinah droned, already bored with the topic.

"This is totally different, Dinah. This is going to be the biggest thing since ... since ... I don't know! Everyone's going to get one."

"Well, you ain't going to see me in that line."

"How come?" Bessie's eyes flared with an odd combination of shock and defensiveness.

Dinah shook her head again. "Because I don't want to be following a fad." Bessie wiped the onion ring grease off her lips, barely concealing her indignation. "Our society is all about fitting in," Dinah continued, "and anyone who stands out is labeled a 'freak' or something of that order. Well, I don't care. I'm proud of being a freak."

***

Dinah sat alone at a table at the Paragon Bar in Portland's Pearl District. She sucked Dead Guy Ale from the bottle and scanned the room. The bar was empty. She rolled her eyes. Everyone in the world was probably waiting in line to buy that damn phone.

She paused when she saw the bartender, Josh Mayfield, standing behind the bar, wiping a glass. He had intense blue eyes and a killer smile. Man, he was cute. Josh looked at her and called out, "You want another drink?"

"How about a Hefeweizen?"

"You got it," Josh said. He poured a pint of Hefeweizen into a tall glass. "You're here all alone?" he asked as he came around to her table.

"All my friends are waiting in line to buy that stupid zPhone."

Josh laughed. "I'm sorry to hear that." He placed the beer on Dinah's table. "So why aren't you getting one?"

Dinah couldn't help but feel self-conscious for a minute. Josh made her nervous. She flicked a piece of hair from her face. "I don't want to follow a trend. I want to be my own person. What about you? Are you going to buy one of those things?"

Josh smiled. "I don't know. Maybe," he replied. "I heard they don't get good battery life." He picked up two empty glasses from her table and cradled them in his arm. "So you're going to just drink here all night long?"

"I guess."

"Well, at least this is cheaper than buying one of those phones."

Dinah laughed. "Tell me about it. I've got enough bills to pay … my phone bill, my tuition, my textbooks…"

"Yeah, I know the feeling. I'm in college too. What are you studying?"

"Nursing," Dinah replied, smiling. It felt good to talk to someone who actually seemed interested. "What about you?" she asked.

"Computer Science. I want to make a lot of money," Josh replied. "I want to, at least, be living in something other than a cardboard box by the time I pay off my tuition and school bills."

Dinah laughed. She glanced at him. She felt lost in his eyes and had to fight the urge to stare.

"Do you mind?" Josh asked as he pulled out the chair and sat down before Dinah could respond. "I'm Josh by the way."

Dinah felt her cheeks burn. It had been a long time since she felt a connection with a complete stranger. Sure, she was attractive. Her wavy black hair, high cheekbones, emerald green eyes. She got hit on all the time, but there was something different about Josh. He actually seemed interested in what she had to say. "I'm Dinah," she said stumbling over her words.

***

Josh nodded and took a gulp of beer. "What about majoring in philosophy? Who the fuck would want to major in that?"

Dinah chuckled. She couldn't remember the last time she had met someone who seemed to be on the same page.

Josh continued. "Has there ever been an employer who's said, 'Man, we're having all kinds of problems. I wish we had someone on our team who could reference and draw conclusions from the story of Siddhartha and also pull up our fourth quarter numbers?'"

Dinah burst out laughing. "I took many philosophy classes and it involved reading and smoking a shit-pile of weed."

"But can we both agree that Latin is the worst major? I mean, no one speaks the language anymore."

"Yeah, but you could impress all the ladies with the Latin etymology of every word," Dinah pointed out.

"While making them their sandwich at Subway?"

Dinah doubled over and slapped her hand on her knees. "You're funny," she giggled.

Josh shook his head in amazement and ran his hand through his hair. "Sometimes I'm amazed by the choices students make."

"My best friend Bessie is a Communications major."

"Oh, brother. That's like the major for anyone who wants to graduate but wants to get totally wasted on weekdays."

Dinah nodded, fingering the lip of her glass with a perfectly manicured digit. "She tells me that the communications classes always smell like dried semen and booze."

Josh laughed. He looked at Dinah; her intense green eyes seemed to be drawing him closer to her. "What are you doing tomorrow?"

"Nothing much, why?" She swallowed a lump in her throat and shifted in her chair.

"Do you want to go out?"

Her heart pounded. She smiled. "I'd love to."

"Great!" Josh smiled.

Dinah looked at her watch. "Well, I better get going. Should I just meet you here tomorrow?"

"That would be perfect. I get off work at seven."

"All right, you have a good night."

"You too, Dinah."

Dinah walked out the door with a skip to her step. Nothing could wipe the smile off her face. And then she stopped dead in her tracks into what appeared to be World War III. People passed on either side of her, talking loudly on their new zPhones. Cars slid and meandered all over the roads as drivers concentrated on their zPhones. A white Toyota Corolla crashed into a restaurant across the street, setting it on fire.

Dinah ran back in the bar not knowing what else to do. Josh was at the far end of the bar sweeping the floor.

He looked up with a perplexed look on his face. "I thought our date was tomorrow," he said with a smile.

"I can't get to my car," Dinah said.

He propped his chin on the broom handle. "What do you mean? Where did you park?"

"I parked in the Smart Park garage on 4th and Yamhill."

"Why did you park all the way over there?"

"It's cheaper to park there. This area's fucking expensive." While she tried to keep her mind on the chaos outside she couldn't keep her eyes from darting to his flexed biceps. Never would she have thought a man with a broom could be so sexy.

"Such a cheapskate," Josh said, smiling.

"But seriously, Josh. There are some crazy people out there. Look outside."

Josh leaned the broom against the bar and walked to a nearby window. His gaze scanned all the carnage.

Dinah stood beside him, stunned by the hoard of people on zPhones. Cars and buildings were on fire and no one seemed to care. No one helped and no one called for help. The police and fire departments were helpless as they, too, were busying talking on zPhones.

Josh ran to the entrance of the bar and locked the door. He poured a shot of Jack Daniel's and gulped it in one fell swoop. Then, he jumped behind the bar and emerged from the counter holding a shotgun.

"A shotgun?" Dinah asked. Though she'd been terrified by what was going on outside, Josh was blowing this a bit out of proportion.

Josh opened one of the cabinet doors and took out a baseball bat. He placed it on the counter. "Take this," he instructed.

"Josh, I don't know …" Dinah stared at the bat and shook her head. She no longer knew where she was safest. Out there with *them* or in here with a …

"Whatever you do, just aim for the head," Josh said as he started filling his pockets with grenades, ninja stars, and bullets.

"Why do you have all of these weapons?" Dinah asked stunned. Why couldn't she find a normal guy?

Josh leaned against the bar. "I should have known this would happen. You know what today is?"

"Tuesday?" She wasn't quite sure what answer he was looking for.

"No, Dinah. Today's the day of the apocalypse," Josh replied.

Dinah took a few steps backwards, lengthening the gap between them. What a crazy bastard. And to think she was starting to really like him. "What are you talking about?"

"What's the date?" he asked, pouring himself another shot of whiskey.

She hesitated, trying to find the significance in the day's date. "June 6th?"

"And the year?" he asked, taking the shot.

For crying out loud, the idiot didn't know what year it was? "2006?" she replied.

"6/6/06. Three sixes!"

"Well, there's a zero before the last six. So technically…"

Josh rambled on, his eyes widening. "Dinah, this is the beginning of the end."

Dinah stared at him. "Are you drunk?"

"Buzzed," he replied with a wink.

"I think I should leave," she said as she slowly headed for the door.

"Wait, don't go out that door!" Josh exclaimed. "Let me take you to your car."

"You have a car?"

"No, I take public transportation," he replied. He looked outside and watched as a city bus zigzagged through the crowd, swerved, then flipped over and caught on fire. "Holy shit," he said under his breath.

"Fine, you can come with me. God, this is ludicrous," Dinah said.

"Okay, well we should …" He was interrupted by heavy knocking on the door.

"We want in!" the people outside yelled. "We want in!"

"Holy barnacles, they're coming in!" Josh exclaimed. zPhone users peeked through the windows, and then someone punched through the glass.

Dinah jumped. Josh grabbed her by the arm and pulled her toward the door. "Ready?" Josh asked as he clutched his shotgun.

Dinah's hands shook but she managed to take some practice swings with the bat. Her heart was racing, adrenaline pumping. It was do or die. "Batter up," she replied.

Josh kicked the door opened and immediately started firing the shotgun at the zPhone users. Blood splattered all over the place.

"Come on! Let's go!" Josh cried out to Dinah.

Dinah felt sick to her stomach. Someone grabbed her hair and was pulling her down. Josh fired, blood splattering all over her clothes, her ears deaf from the shot.

"You're okay," Josh whispered in her ear. "We need to go." He grabbed Dinah's hand and she followed him into the zPhone abyss.

The entire city of Portland was falling apart. Fires blazed everywhere. People lay sprawled on the streets and sidewalks dying. None of the destruction caught the attention of a single zPhone user as they walked aimlessly down the streets, oblivious to what was going on around them.

Dinah and Josh darted through the chaos and headed toward the parking garage. Dinah stopped suddenly.

"What are you doing?" Josh asked.

Dinah stared at Bessie who was busy talking on a zPhone. Josh aimed his shotgun for her head.

"Josh, wait!" Dinah cried.

Josh wiped blood off his face. "Wait for what?"

"Don't shoot her. That's my best friend!" Dinah replied. She took a step closer to Bessie. Bessie's eyes were fixated to the Internet on the zPhone. She looked up and stared blankly at Dinah.

"It's me, Dinah. Dinah Nash. Do you remember me, Bessie?"

"My video games, can record and track e-mails, recording games, nice weather, want stock market report, play games, games and ..." Bessie's eyes were glazed over and her pupils were dilated as she sputtered gibberish. It was all incomprehensible.

"Bessie!" Dinah cried out.

"Traffic reports and e-mails. Cool screen. Video games. Buy stock. Weather's nice. Games and my e-mails. See my page. See ..." Gibberish continued to spew from Bessie.

"No!" Dinah screamed. She should have stopped her. She should have kept her from getting the stupid phone.

"It's too late," Josh said. "You must do what's right."

Bessie held out the zPhone for Dinah to grab. "Games and e-mail..."

Dinah knew Josh was right. She whispered, "I'm sorry, Bessie," closed her eyes, and blindly swung her baseball bat right at Bessie's skull. A home run. Bessie fell to the ground—her zPhone hit the curb and broke in half.

Dinah wailed, screamed, saw her friend dead in the road and couldn't stop the tears. She fell to her knees.

Josh did his best to console her. "You did the right thing," he said. "Let's get to your car. We're almost there."

"No," Dinah said.

Josh glared at her in disbelief. "No?"

She stood, wiped the tears from her cheek and gritted her teeth. "We have to destroy the root of the zPhone. I don't want anyone else to get hurt."

31

Josh nodded. "Where would the root be?"

Dinah looked up. "Pioneer Place."

Pioneer Place was an upscale, urban shopping mall in downtown Portland. The mall was spread out between four buildings interconnected by skywalks. It was always bustling with shoppers who had nothing better to do then buy to their heart's content. As Josh and Dinah entered the mall, several zPhone users meandered past stores.

They ran inside a Brookstone to hide. No one ever shopped there so they were assured safety.

"Where are people buying these zPhones?" Josh asked.

"Downstairs in the Grape Computers store," she replied.

Josh nodded then rubbed his forearm over his sweaty forehead. "When we get in, what are we going to do?"

Dinah looked at him with conviction. "We're going to destroy every single last one of those damn phones."

Josh looked at her and leaned in closer. "You know something, Dinah. This has been one hell of a first date."

She smiled back, charmed by the laughter in his eyes. "I like you."

"I like you, too." He shoved a grenade in his pocket and reached out to push the hair off her face.

Dinah tilted her head into his hands. He snaked his fingers to the nape of her neck and tugged her closer. Josh brought his lips to hers, and she wanted to forget everything about zPhones and simply lose herself in his kiss.

Josh pulled away and hungrily licked his lips. "We have a job to do," he whispered.

"Yeah," she replied with a sigh. She shook away the warm sensation of his lips and brought her attention back to the task at hand. "You ready to go kick some zPhone ass?"

"Hell, yeah." Josh grinned and reloaded his shotgun. As they ran out of the Brookstone, Josh and Dinah started killing zPhone users with the swing of a bat and the pull of a trigger. Phones flew into the air only to crash and splinter into pieces on the shining floor as their users collapsed. A few screams could be heard, but for the most part, zPhoners—those who were still alive— just kept the phone to their ears until a gunshot ended their call. Josh and Dinah ran down the escalator and headed toward the Grape Store.

The Grape Store was swamped with people waiting in line to receive their new zPhone. Several Grape Store employees looked at Dinah and Josh and nodded a greeting.

"Hi, welcome to the Grape Store," one of them said.

Dinah smashed her baseball bat into that employee's face while the other employees stared at them.

"Someone call the cops!" one exclaimed.

"Oh, no you don't mother fuckers!" Josh fired his shotgun around the store. People fell one after the other and the few Josh didn't attain with a bullet, Dinah caught with her swinging bat.

With no phone to occupy them, many retaliated and came after them.

Dinah looked over at Josh when his gun fell silent.

"What the fuck are you doing? Shoot! These fuckers are fighting back!" She whacked a guy who lunged at her. "Shoot before they take over!"

"I'm out of bullets!" Josh screamed. "I have to reload."

"Have you seen this latest zPhone?" an employee said to Josh, holding up the shiny new object.

Josh stared at the zPhone and was momentarily blinded by its clear screen and cool color. "Dinah!" he called out in panic. He could feel his willpower ebbing away and the sales guy was moments away from convincing him to buy the damn thing.

Dinah turned to see the trouble Josh was in. The glaze that was coming over Josh was frightening.

"Dinah! Help!" Josh exclaimed.

Dinah ran toward him, shouting a battle cry, and swinging with vengeance. The bat made solid contact with the employee's skull and knocked his jaw off.

"Oh my God. They almost had me, Dinah. Thanks."

While Dinah kept the remainder of shoppers and employees at bay, Josh reloaded and was soon firing off one bullet after another. After much bloodshed, everyone in the store was on the floor dead or dying. Dinah ran behind the counter and grabbed all of the zPhones from the display. One by one, she smashed them with her baseball bat, shouting with glee as they split, cracked, and shattered.

"We did it," Dinah shouted. "Josh, we got them all." She looked up and didn't see Josh. "Josh? Where are you?"

Suddenly, she saw Josh on the other side of the store near the entrance to the stockroom. He was smiling and ogling a phone being shown to him by a pretty Grape Computer employee.

"No! Josh!" Dinah exclaimed.

"Dinah." Josh held a silver and black phone up for her to see. "This phone … it's so powerful. It's got a 5 megapixel camera and…"

"Josh! Put the phone down, Josh."

"Wi-Fi, satellite radio, voice recording … Dinah I must get one. This thing is way too cool. I can't help it. It's got a tip calculator!"

"You don't need that!" Dinah screamed.

"It's so shiny and cool. Look at these sleek lines. Look at this screen."

"No! No! No!" Dinah cried.

"You must get one of these." Josh had an idiot's grin on his face as he reached into his pocket and handed a few bills to the employee.

Dinah dropped the baseball bat on the counter and ran to the employee. She tackled the petite blonde to the floor. She punched her pretty little face and laughed as blood splattered on her already bloodstained shirt.

Josh looked at her in horror and shook his head. "Dinah? What are you doing? She was just trying to…"

"Are you okay?" Dinah asked trying to catch her breath.

Josh blinked and shook his head before looking at the blonde on the floor. "Yeah," he mumbled. "Yeah, I'm fine. What happened? What did she…? What did I…?"

"You were about to buy one of those phones."

"Holy finger fuck." He looked at the zPhone in his hand and let it drop with disdain. "You saved my life." He bent down and grabbed the money from her dead blonde's hand. "I might need this for something *really* important."

Dinah smiled with relief. She grabbed him, pulled him close and planted a hot, wet kiss on his stunned lips. "Let me get my baseball bat from behind the counter and then we can get out of here and head to my car."

"I'm gonna make a quick run to the men's room and I'll meet you in the parking lot."

Dinah frowned. "I'll come with you. It can be dangerous."

"Don't be ridiculous. I'll be fine."

They went their separate ways. Dinah knocked people left and right, swinging her bat as if trying to get candy from a piñata. When she reached the parking garage, she searched for her car, her footsteps measured and quick.

She heard someone running toward her. She turned around, bat in hand, ready to attack.

Josh emerged from the darkness with a somewhat mischievous grin on his face.

"Told you I'd be fine." He hugged her and kissed her temple.

"What are you grinning about? What are you up to?"

"Nothing. This has been such an unforgettable night," Josh said. "I'm happy."

Dinah flashed him a warm and affectionate smile.

"You know, I really like your smile," he said. "And the way you make me smile."

"Thank you," was all Dinah could muster. She closed her eyes, pinched her arm, expecting to awake from a dream, but Josh was still standing before her. He pulled her close and kissed her. It felt like electricity surged throughout her body. "Dinah?" Josh said.

"Yes?" she cooed.

"You have to check out this zPhone, it's really cool." He pulled the zPhone from his pocket.

Dinah stepped back, shocked, shaking her head. "Where did you get that?"

"I found one that was still working even after you smashed it with your bat. Look at this, it has a compass."

Dinah grabbed the zPhone and was about to shatter it to pieces. But she stared at it. Her eyes felt funny, as if she couldn't blink. Her body went numb. "Wow...this is pretty cool."

"It's got Bluetooth," Josh added.

"Maybe I should have gotten one before shattering them all," she said.

"Yeah. Oh well, I'm sure we can get them online."

"Can it play MP3s?"

"MP3s and TV shows."

"Way too cool."

unemployment oregon

"Unemployment is capitalism's way of getting you to plant a garden."
Orson Scott Card

While people enjoyed the sun at beautiful Cannon Beach, I sat in my boss's windowless office, waiting for him to come in.

My boss, Mr. Peabody, was a micromanaging maniac. He wanted to control everything— a real annoying bastard. And, most of the time, what he said was just plain garbage.

It was sad to think that I spent most of my adult life with this jerk. In fact, I didn't like anyone in the office. They were all jerks. Six years ago, I graduated from the University of Portland and landed this job. Met a girl. Got married. Somehow, I managed to fall into the working mold: get up, go to work, come home, go to sleep. Repeat.

Peabody walked in and took a seat behind his desk. He looked like a cross between E.T. and Jay Leno. I was almost positive that he got trapped in his locker by bullies back in high school. This was his way of getting revenge ... by being a jackass.

He looked at me. "Mr. Buchanan, how are you doing?"

"Doing well," I replied.

"Good ... good. Well, as you know, we are taking a major financial hit due to Wall Street. And, in an effort to reduce costs, we are restructuring our business, and that will result in the elimination of a number of positions in our company. Unfortunately, your position has been selected, and it is with great sadness that I'm going to have to lay you off. Today will be your last day of work with us, and we have information to share with you regarding your severance package, COBRA, and unemployment insurance. I know this is a lot of information coming to you at once, and I'm so sorry to have to relay this message to you. Before I go any further, I want to see how you're doing. Are you okay?"

I was shocked. Not that I was getting laid off, but shocked by the amount of bullshit that flew out of his mouth. He was sad to see me go? Please. He didn't even know my name a week ago, and I had slaved at this company for six fucking years!

"Mr. Buchanan, are you okay?" Peabody asked again.

"I'm fine," I replied. The amount of bullshit was startling. "Am I the only one who's being laid off in my department? Why me?"

"Yes, yours is the only position in our department that's being eliminated. Again, please don't feel that you've disappointed anyone. I want you to know that you could be considered for rehire once the hiring freeze is lifted. For now though, understand that we had to eliminate one position, and, purely from a functional standpoint, your position made the most sense." Peabody had a horrible habit of smacking his lips when he talked.

I nodded. *Whatever.*

"I just want to thank you for all your hard work and dedication for the past six years. You have made it a better place around here, and I'm personally going to miss working with you. Thank you for all that you've done for us."

It was a better place around here? He'd missed me? Ah man, the bullshit machine must be on full force today. I got up from my chair, shook that weasel's hand, and walked out.

At first, I was disappointed. Great, now I was going to have to write resumes, send them out, and wait for the rejection letters. This was going to suck.

But then, as I felt the warmth of the sun along with the ocean breeze, it hit me like a ton of bricks. I was free. Free from being controlled by people I could not stand. I felt an immense weight lift off my shoulders as I walked to the car, and I rode a wave of euphoria all the way home.

***

I was still basking in my newfound freedom when I entered my house. I grabbed a bottle of Widmer beer, sat down on the couch, and watched ESPN. I had nothing else better to do, and life seemed perfect.

Suddenly, I heard my wife, Karen, walk down the stairs. "You're home?" Needless to say, she was surprised to see me. "What happened?"

I told her the great news, but she didn't quite see it my way. Her brow furrowed and she made the "sad" face—the face that meant the tears were coming. But, no tears came.

"I'm so sorry to hear that," she said. She sat down on the armrest, rubbing my head. She leaned in to kiss my forehead and her long dark hair hung in front of my face, blocking my view of the TV. "Well, you'll find another job."

I looked at her like she'd gone crazy. "Find another job?"

"Yeah. I can help you out. I know some good websites you can go to find job openings."

"I don't think I want another job right now," I told her.

She straightened up and pointed to the stack of unopened envelopes on the kitchen table. "How are you planning on paying those bills?" She sighed and stared off into space. I hated when she did that. She was starting to put a damper on my enthusiasm, and her tone of voice had taken on some elevation. I thought about asking her to bring me another beer, but my self-preservation instinct kicked in. My mind was racing faster than the beer was slipping down my throat.

"I could win the lottery," I replied. I quickly started listing off all the things I could do if I won a few million.

"What's wrong with you?" she screamed, pulling me from my reverie. She had managed to close in on my personal space, but wasn't blocking the TV anymore. Thank God for that.

"You better have a plan to get out of this," she said.

Her eyes were starting to turn red at the corners, and her hands had found a solid resting place on her hips.

"I'll think of something," I said. *Yeah, right.*

"You better find another job real quick," she said as she headed for the bedroom.

I loved her, but sometimes, I just couldn't stand her. She was very controlling. When we met, she was this cute, bubbly twenty-something who was responsible but craved adventure. But somehow, things over the years changed. She hardened over the edges. Her worries were buying a house in a good neighborhood, or what life insurance plan we should invest in. She worked as a secretary at a company that produced and sold luggage. She answered calls. She answered e-mails. She answered to her boss. She answered to everyone in the office. She was essentially a slave wearing a pencil skirt and pumps. I felt kind of sorry for her. No wonder she was so demanding at home. She had to have some kind of power somewhere.

***

Two days later, I applied for unemployment benefits. I was amazed at how much money the government was going to give me for doing nothing. Sure, I had to fill out an online survey every week, but I could just breeze and lie through those answers. *Did you fail to accept an offer of work last week?* No. *Were you away from your permanent residence for more than 3 days last week?* Nope. *Did you actively look for work last week?* Duh, of course. I waited a couple of days, and the check was sent. Sure, I could only get 26 weeks worth of checks but, for me, it was 26 weeks worth of freedom.

I had worked hard for the past six years for my past employer. I had money saved up. Fresh out of college, the benefits seemed amazing, and I couldn't turn it down. But was it worth it?

I walked out of my house and went down to walk along Cannon Beach. On weekends, this beach was always crowded with employed folks looking for some relaxation. But today, Tuesday, there was hardly anyone here. The herd of Saturday sun worshippers and Sunday swimmers were at work. They were being yelled at by their retarded bosses and were being corralled into tiny, cramped, and noisy workstations.

I scanned the glistening sand. I practically had the whole beach to myself. I looked out on the horizon and watched the waves crash on the shore. With a can of soda in one hand and a fistful of Frito-Lays in the other, I leaned back and took in the sun.

***

Later in the day, I took a road trip to Portland and rode my bike along the many bridges. In addition, I took a trip on the Portland Spirit Cruise and went fishing on the Willamette. Hell, I even got to check out the grave of Bobbie the Wonder Dog. I had visited Portland several times in my lifetime, and did all the touristy things. But there was something different about today. Clear skies, crisp air, and I was a free man.

Later, I went to Barnaby's Restaurant in downtown Portland. I saw plenty of men in suits and ties. I was so glad that I didn't have to wear that shit anymore. The shorts I'd jumped into that morning were ten times more comfortable than any suit. And my flip-flops... I didn't care if they'd paid three hundred bucks for their fancy leather loafers—no one was more comfortable than I was.

After a nice, unhurried lunch, I strolled around town before making the drive back home. I grabbed a beer from the fridge, flopped down on the comfy couch and watched SportsCenter. I drank a Corona and watched the results from that day's golf tournament.

Karen walked in just as I was about to flip channels. She was dressed in a nice white skirt with a pale pink button down blouse. Though she looked real professional, she also looked sweaty and hot. She kicked out of her four-inch heels and slipped into her flip-flops. I felt so sorry for her.

"Hi, honey," I said.

She looked at me then glanced at my bike gear. "What did you do today?"

"I rode my bike around Portland. I haven't done that in ages."

"Did you check out Monster.com? Careerbuilder.com? Craigslist?"

Looking for another job was the furthest thing from my mind since losing the last one. I had planned on spending the summer drinking heavily and dancing naked with my wife. Remaining stress-free can extend your life.

"I checked out Craigslist."

"Oh, good. Any good jobs there?"

I looked at her funny. "No, I was looking for Eddie Vedder tickets. He's playing at the Hooker Creek Event Center in Redmond."

"So you didn't look for a job?"

"Was I supposed to?"

She rolled her eyes. "You are such an ass sometimes, you know that?"

I got up to leave the house.

Karen grabbed me by the arm and scowled. "Where are you going?"

"I'm going barhopping. Want to come?"

"On a Tuesday night?" Her eyes showed reserved interest, but she quickly packed that away and put on her indignant glare. "I have work tomorrow."

"Oh, that's too bad." I walked out of the house.

***

The next day I woke up feeling a little tense between the shoulder blades, so I decided to get a massage. I hadn't had one in ages. Man, it felt incredible! Then I took a field trip to Multnomah Falls and hiked all the way up the mountain. Not only was the view absolutely amazing, but the complete sense of freedom was downright intoxicating. Later in the day, I walked past Guitar Center in Seaside, strolled in, picked up a Fender Electric, strummed a few chords, and bought it on the spot. I always wanted to learn how to play, and I always wanted to be in a rock band. Now I'd have time to pursue that dream.

When I got home, Karen greeted me with an unexpected grin. What had happened? Had she quit her job? Was she now going to join me on my daily escapades? A moment of excitement was quickly followed by a huge sense of loss. While I loved her madly, spending day-after-day traipsing around Cannon Beach with her in tow would surely turn sour.

"What's up?" I asked.

"Well, I talked to my boss. He wants to talk to you tomorrow about a job opening!" She clapped and giggled.

While she was about to burst open from excitement, my heart was about to fall apart and hit the floor in a bloody mess. "What's the job?"

"You would be a sales representative."

Sales? Yuck. What a terrible job. Selling shitty products to people with brains the size of walnuts could drive a man insane. In this case, I would be selling luggage. God, sounded like a wonderful job. I could sell luggage to people heading off on vacation and listen to them go on and on… Yawn.

"Really?" I tried to sound enthusiastic, but only managed disbelief.

"Yes! Now, come on and get some rest. Tomorrow's going to be a big day for you!" She patted me on the back and guided me to the bedroom.

I'd been having wonderful, stress-free sleep these past few nights. Tonight, I was sure to have one nightmare after the other.

***

In the morning I dressed up in a suit, tie, and a nice pair of slacks. I looked and felt like such a stiff. This was definitely interrupting my leisure time. But then again, it would make Karen happy. And a content woman would do pleasing things.

"You sure look nice, sweetie. I'm so happy to see you're taking the job interview seriously."

"Of course I take it seriously. Why shouldn't I?"

She smiled and patted my clean-shaven cheek. "I'm going to pick up some dry cleaning, so you go ahead, and maybe I'll see you there. Maybe we can have lunch together and celebrate your new position."

"Sure thing, honey." I walked out with her, happy to see her so happy.

"I better go." She gave me a kiss and left, heading to the east. "Good luck."

With her out of sight, I took off my suit and tie, revealing the cool tie-dyed shirt I'd bought the week before from a surfer dude by the beach. Then I pulled down my slacks, revealing the camo shorts I'd put on underneath, hopped on my bike and headed to her place of employment for the interview.

I really had absolutely no intention of getting hired, but I was available for free entertainment.

I walked into the building and headed for the young, curly-haired receptionist. She slid open the glass partition. "Can I help you?"

"Yeah, I'm John Buchanan. I'm here to see Mr. Andrew Coulon for the sales position."

"All right, please have a seat, and I'll let Mr. Coulon know you're here."

At this point, I wondered why she needed to inform Mr. Coulon. I already had an appointment. These were the little details that made me question the meaning of life, but I took a seat on the nearest couch and waited for the next event to take place.

I casually flipped through a magazine, passing the time looking at travel articles. I could not believe Karen worked here. It was so...rigid. I heard the gentle clip-clop of fashionable high heels and, like any red-blooded guy, looked up to catch a glimpse. I was not disappointed. I saw the sexiest woman on the planet and, my God, she was walking straight toward me. Her long blonde hair flowed down her back and brushed across her beautiful behind. I was in pure heaven.

"Mr. Buchanan?" Her sultry voice added to her physical beauty.

"That's me."

"I'm Sabrina, Mr. Coulon's assistant. I'll be taking notes during your interview with him. He's ready for you in his office. Would you like me to grab you some coffee?"

I couldn't stop looking at her body. Her breasts were barely contained in that blue dress.

"I'm good, thanks." I swallowed the engorged lump in my throat and smiled. I knew I was staring at her like some third grader who'd seen his first pair of boobs. I tried to stop, I really did, but my eyes just couldn't let go of those boobs.

If she noticed my adolescent admiration, she didn't let on. She led me, and I cheerfully followed her to Mr. Coulon's office. My father had always said I would never be a leader, but I sure knew how to follow. And, with a view like that up front, who wanted to lead anyway?

Inside the office, Mr. Coulon was sitting in his leather chair. I looked out the window, which had a nice view of downtown Seaside.

"Mr. Coulon," Sabrina said, "this is John Buchanan."

Mr. Coulon stood and shook my hand. Boy did he look out of it. He had every imaginable sign of stress on his face. His hair was as gray as my father's wool sweater. This man looked like he was all about business and no fun.

"Have a seat," he told me.

I took a seat. I looked at Sabrina who took the chair beside me and crossed her legs. I felt like I was in the movie *Basic Instinct*. How could Mr. Coulon be so stressed when he had such a sexy fox for an assistant?

"Karen has told me a lot about you. It sounds like you have a lot of experience in sales."

"I do," I replied, wiping the drool from the corner of my mouth.

"Tell me a little about yourself," Mr. Coulon said.

"Well, I've spent the last six years doing computer software sales, a little bit of marketing as well, although not too much. I think I would be an asset to your office, and I still have most of my teeth."

My last comment got a smile from Sabrina, but not from Mr. Coulon. Man, he needed to lighten up.

"So, why should I hire you?" he asked.

"I have excellent customer service skills, I can close sales very well, and I do a courtesy flush."

I looked at Sabrina, who smiled again. She was scribbling something on the writing pad. There was no stopping me when I had a captive audience. I allowed my knee to brush against her thigh as I waited for the next stupid question.

"Where do you see yourself in five years?"

"Sitting in your office."

"I see, very ambitious individual," he said. "It took me ten long years of hard work and dedication to get where I am right now."

"Did you ever do anything fun during that time?" I asked.

He scrunched his face, his wrinkles more pronounced. "Well, of course. I golfed. I read books. I went to parties."

"Parties? Like what, raves and nightclubs?" I asked him, jokingly of course. I looked at Sabrina. She now had her hand over her mouth and was working hard to hold back a laugh.

"No, like business gatherings," he replied. He cleared his throat.

Real exciting. This guy was the life of the party. "But enough about me," he said, "tell me, Mr. Buchanan, what do you consider is your greatest strength?"

I looked straight into his bloodshot eyes. "I know how to live life to the fullest."

"What is your greatest weakness?" he asked.

I couldn't believe he'd ask another question. My God, when was this going to end?

"I totally suck at *Mario Kart*. I mean, I get so far ahead of everyone and then BAM! Fucking blue shell hits me right before I cross the finish line. Damn cheating blue shells."

Sabrina laughed and Mr. Coulon directed a disappointed glare at her. He then turned to me. "What's that?" he asked.

"*Mario Kart*? It's only the greatest video game ever created. God, you need to get out more."

Mr. Coulon got up and shook my hand. "Thank you for coming in. I'll let you know if you get the job."

Sabrina escorted me to the door.

***

Two weeks went by, and I hadn't received a call about the job. How disappointing. Well, not really, but whatever. I was sitting at home, watching *Jeopardy!* when Karen bounded through the door. She was ecstatic.

"Honey! Guess what?" she cried out in euphoria.

"You're pregnant?" I asked.

"No, I'm the new boss! I'm taking over for Mr. Coulon. He stepped down. I guess all that hard work really paid off."

I smiled. "Did he say why?"

"He said he needed to spend more time outside of work," she replied. "He's been working pretty hard, especially this past year. But, oh my God! We have to celebrate!"

"Congratulations, darling," I said.

"My first order of business ... I'm going to hire you as my top sales guy. I'll make sure you get all the best leads. What do you say?" She hopped onto the couch, leaned in to peck me on the cheek then bounced back onto the couch. Tigger would appear to be on valium next to this woman.

I looked at her. "So, you'll be my boss?"

She laughed. "I guess I would, yes."

"Well, I'm afraid I'm going to have to turn it down."

She looked at me with a combination of puzzlement and resentment. "What?" she whined.

"I'm turning down your offer."

"Did you get another job?" she asked.

"No," I quickly replied.

"Then you better have a Plan B!" she screamed at me.

"I do," I replied. "I'm going on a trip to New Zealand. Never been there before. Want to come?"

"I can't. I'm working."

"Oh ... that's too bad." I walked out the door. The night was fresh, not a cloud in the sky. It hadn't rained in Cannon Beach since I got laid off.

Poor Karen, she really should consider going with me to New Zealand. It would be a lot of fun.

Oh well, I guess it'll be just me and Mr. Coulon then.

Doing the Right Thing

"Run like hell and get the agony over with."

Clarence DeMar

As I walked into the office for an early morning meeting with my agent to discuss my latest book, I saw a young man standing on a ledge just outside the window seemingly ready to jump to his death. We were on the top floor of one of the taller buildings in Portland, so his fall would certainly be fatal.

I shuffled closer, afraid to make any noise. And then I asked him, "What on Earth are you doing?"

He turned his head abruptly—a scowl on his face—as if I had just interrupted something important. "What does it look like I'm doing? I'm about to jump," he snapped. His hands nervously worked the frayed edges of his sleeves, his fingers never stopping for a second.

"Why?"

"Because it's the … oh hell. What business is it of yours anyways? Do you mind going on your way and leaving me to it?"

"I really can't. I have a meeting here."

His forehead crinkled. A piece of his scraggily brown hair fell over his eyes. His fingernails were dirty.

"What's your name?" I asked.

"Jackson," he replied. Judging from his attire, he was probably the building's janitor. A brown jumpsuit, wrinkled and worn, grease stains blotched the legs and arms.

"Jackson, I'm Arran. Nice to meet you." I took a few steps closer but kept my distance. I wasn't qualified in any way to help him, but I couldn't just leave and let him jump. "Can you tell me what's wrong?"

"Nothing."

"Well, something must be wrong if you're standing on the ledge of a tall building thinking about falling to your impending doom."

Jackson paused for a second. His eyes flickered. "I hate myself."

"Don't say that."

"You don't even know my story," Jackson replied. "I hate myself so much. I hated things before. Then it started to get a little better until something happened the other day and now I can't live with myself. It's not like I want to leave this world. I just want to leave myself. And I'm having panic attacks. I can't sleep or eat. I feel sick. I'm crying. I can't look at myself. And I just want it all to end. I hate myself so much." He turned his head toward the ground, his shoulders heaving.

What could I possibly say to make him feel better? I swallowed the lump in my throat. "Can you tell me more about what happened and why you want to commit suicide?"

"I can't. It's just …"

"I know it hurts a lot right now, and it seems like there's no way out. I believe I can help you, if you let me." I had no idea how I could help him, but I was grasping at straws. The poor guy was a mess, ready to take the plunge.

"What can you do? I'm ready to leave this earth now!" Jackson angrily replied.

"I can get you some help right now. How would you like to proceed?"

"I'm done with all of this!"

"I understand. You see no hope. But I do. You need to come with me right now," I said compassionately. I reached out my hand. "Look, I don't know your story, but I don't really care. I care about you. And I'm sure I'm not the only person who cares about you. You seem young. How old are you?"

"Twenty-five."

"That's about the same age I was when I thought about suicide," I lied. "My girlfriend had left me. I thought life was hopeless without her. I just didn't want to go on. It hurt too much."

"Really?" He pursed his lips.

"Yes, Jackson, really. So I thought about how I could kill myself. Getting hit by a car. Overdosing on drugs. Jumping off a building. But then I realized something: I could change. And look at where I am today … a writer who's about to get another book published. Look, I know life has got you down in the dumps and there's a ton of weight on your shoulders, but let me help you."

Jackson nodded, then hesitantly walked inside the meeting room. A group of onlookers had gathered at the door and they applauded when Jackson set foot inside. Thank God. I couldn't have a man's suicide on my conscience.

***

The next day, I was sitting in my living room, listening to local conservative pundit Lars Larson talk about Jackson on the radio. I stared at the wall, stunned.

"This is Lars Larson. Have you seen Jackson Edwards? Call Lars Larson of the Lars Larson Show. 1-866-HEY-LARS or larslarson@larslarson.com."

They just announced there was a warrant out for Jackson's arrest. Apparently, he was a suspect in a series of gruesome murders around the city. My throat clenched.

My wife Ally walked into the room and paused to listen to the radio. She glanced at me.

How the fuck was I supposed to know that was the reason he hated himself so much? The guy was a freaking psychopath. A schizo. A lunatic. If I had known, I would have pushed him off that ledge.

Ally turned off the radio. "Isn't that the guy you saved?"

That's right, I thought. Rub it in. I did one good deed in my life and it turned around to bite me. I looked up into her pretty hazel eyes and was happy to see empathy and not reproach.

"Yup," I replied, then took a sip of my Hefewizen. "I thought I was doing the right thing."

"Well, how could you have known?" She sat on the arm of the couch and leaned her elbow on my back.

"That is the last time I ever help a suicidal man. From now on, if they are going to jump or shoot themselves or hang themselves, I'm going to just sit there and say, 'Go ahead.'"

"You're just going to watch them die?" Ally's eyes widened.

"I'll cover my eyes," I assured her. "Hell, I'm not going to help anyone anymore. If an old lady wants help crossing the street, I'll tell her to go fuck herself. You never know, I could be helping a future rapist."

Ally laughed. "Now you're just being ridiculous." She threw a Blockbuster Video rental box on my lap. "Honey, when you go to the grocery store, could you drop that movie off at Blockbuster?"

I looked at the movie on my lap. "God, this movie was awful."

"Well, you aren't a great fan of romantic dramas, so I'm not surprised you didn't like it."

"No, that has nothing to do with it. This was a sorry excuse for a romantic drama. Okay, I may not be a fan, and some of them are tolerable, but this? I mean, the man and woman spend most of the movie exchanging glances or staring longingly at each other. Why do they do that anyways? I mean, when I first met you, I freaked for your long dark hair, and I was nuts about your hot body, but we didn't stare at each other for hours before we finally kissed. Hell, if you stared at me for that long I would have thought there was something on my face."

Ally playfully stared at me. "I love you, sweetheart."

I stared at her as long as I could then turned away. "Stop that!"

***

Later that day, I walked in the Blockbuster Video. Cameron, the customer service representative, stood behind the counter.

"Hi," Cameron said.

"Just wanted to return this movie," I replied.

"*Love in First Gear*? How was it?"

"It's not as bad as you might think. It's actually worse. Much worse," I replied.

Cameron scanned the movie then threw it in the back. He looked at me and smiled. "Mr. Gimba, I wanted to thank you the other day for putting in one thousand dollars towards the marathon," he said.

"Not a problem," I replied. "To be honest, I was surprised at just how little other people were contributing. I mean, don't they care about saving whales?"

"They don't have nearly as much money as you do. I don't think they can put down a thousand dollars per mile."

What? I wanted to shout. A thousand dollars a mile? He had to be mistaken. That was ridiculous. Who the hell gave a thousand bucks a mile?

"Each mile?" I asked, trying to keep the panic from my voice.

"Yes. Each mile I run. You really are quite generous, Mr. Gimba. I hope you don't mind but I contacted the media. I think they'll be very happy to report your unending generosity. You're a true model to all citizens of Portland."

I cleared my throat, coughed, and looked around. How could I argue with that? "Not at all," I finally managed to say. God, I was so nervous. I hadn't read the fine print. I looked at Cameron and tried to gauge his fitness level. He seemed a little heavy. He had some extra flab around his stomach; his arms were flabby. He was probably a slow runner. He'd be sweating and panting within a mile. As I scrutinized him, he eyed me with open admiration. I cleared my throat again and tried to sound cool and aloof. "So, like, how many miles do you think you can run? Probably two or three, right?"

"I've been working extremely hard. I've hired Alberto Salazar as my personal trainer."

"Who's he?"

"Only one of the greatest marathon runners of all time. He won the New York Marathon three times. He's currently coaching some Olympians in Eugene."

Double shit. This was going to cost me a fortune.

"I've been running about a half marathon a day. I'll be ready for the whole thing."

The whole thing? I'd be broke. I'd have to sell my home or my car. The advance on my book would have to go to this shitty marathon. I left Blockbuster feeling defeated.

***

When I got home, I ripped open the fridge, grabbed a beer and guzzled half of it before walking into the living room. I sat down, told Ally what happened, and stared blankly at the television screen.

At first she seemed pissed. Her brow crinkled, her lips tightened. She reclined in the Lazy-Boy and sighed. She flipped through the donation paperwork. "It clearly says here that the donation is per mile."

"I thought it was a thousand dollars for the whole marathon. I didn't know it was per mile," I replied.

"Do you realize if he were to complete the marathon, you would have to pay $26,200?"

"No, $26,000. It's a thousand per mile. I'm not paying him two hundred more. I'll be broke enough as it is if I have to pay such a ridiculous amount."

"Well, just tell him you made a mistake. I'm sure he would understand. I mean that's a lot of money. Surely he realizes that."

"I can't. He's called *The Oregonian*, the *Portland Tribune*, KGW, KATU, all the major media players. He's making me look like some kind of hero." I sat on the sofa and kicked my feet up on the coffee table.

I was angry and didn't care if I scuffed the table's shiny finish. "Why the fuck would anyone want to run a marathon? I mean, do you know how a marathon originated? Phidipides traversed twenty-six hilly miles from Marathon to Athens to give word that the Greeks had defeated the Persians. He collapsed dead right on the spot after delivering that news. Think that's dumb? Think about the second person to run a marathon. At some point, here's his thought process: 'Well, gee. The last guy who tried this lost his life. Hmm. Okay, I'll do it.'"

"You're just upset you have to fork over a thousand per mile. You deserve this. You're a writer. I would think you would read the application carefully."

"And people actually pay to do this? They pay a hundred bucks to wake up at five in the bloody morning and suffer the pain of running that distance! I'd pay a hundred bucks to not have to do that!"

"You're apparently willing to pay more than that to not run." Ally got off her Lazy-Boy and sat down next to me. "If it's any consolation, at least it's going to a good cause."

"A good cause? Yeah, saving the whales. Real good cause."

"Whales need our help."

"Oh, fuck the whales. What have whales done for me lately? Nothing, that's what."

"You better stop your pouting and just accept this. You're not going to be able to get out of this one. Just shut up and pay."

I thought about it for a second. There was no way I was just going to shut up and pay. The organizers couldn't make me pay. I set my beer on the floor and pulled Ally closer to me. I needed to find a way out of this.

***

I returned to Blockbuster Video the next day. Cameron was whistling a monotone tune as he cleaned the store counter. He looked up at me. "Arran! How are you doing?"

"I'm doing all right. Hey, about that marathon..."

"Did you get interviewed yet?"

"Sorry?"

"I was interviewed by KATU this morning. I told them that you were the one who was donating a thousand dollars per mile. I thought they would have interviewed you by now."

"Haven't gotten a call," I said. I leaned against the counter. "How's the training coming along?"

"Very good. I'm up to fifteen miles right now. I'll be at 26.2 in no time. Alberto has been a very good teacher."

"Great, great," I said. "I was watching the news last night and, coincidentally, they were talking about how marathon running isn't that good for you."

"What do you mean?"

"Well, I heard that several hundred people a year die from heart attacks while running these things. And then there's heatstroke and hypothermia. And the after effects … knee injuries, broken feet, it's pretty dangerous."

"You have to be in peak physical condition," Cameron said. "My doctor told me that he's never seen a healthier heart than mine."

"I was thinking, maybe instead of putting in a thousand per mile, I'd just give you three thousand right now. That way, you don't have to train nearly as hard. I don't want you to suffer a heart attack or anything like that."

Cameron ran his hands through his hair. "Mr. Gimba, that is very kind of you. But I'm confident I can do it."

"Four thousand?" I asked.

"Mr. Gimba …"

"Five thousand?"

"I'll be fine," he snapped. "I appreciate your concern. But I'll be okay. Alberto has been monitoring my progress. He'll make sure that I don't work too hard."

Cameron walked around the counter. Should I trip him? Maybe I could break his ankle or something. Nah, I wasn't that evil.

"I really appreciate what you're doing," he said as he put his hand on my shoulder. "I consider you a true friend."

Cameron walked on, rag in hand to wipe down another counter. Great, now I had a friend who worked at Blockbuster Fucking Video. A friendship worth $26,000.

***

It was eight in the morning when Ally nudged me and insisted we go to the Portland Marathon to watch Cameron run.

Run away with my money. Bastard.

The place was packed. Hundreds of onlookers came to watch the race. Didn't anyone have anything better to do on a Sunday morning? I spotted Cameron among the racers. He was at the starting line, stretching and hopping around like some maniac.

Ally held a large "Go Cameron!" sign. "You look great, Cameron!" she cried out. Cameron looked her way and gave a thumbs-up.

"Of course he looks great. He hasn't even started the damn thing," I said to her. "Say that to him when he's on mile twenty-one. Let's see how great he looks then."

"I know you're bitter about the money thing, but at least have a good time," Ally said. She wrapped her arm around my waist.

I looked up into the sky wondering if God was up there watching all of this. I wasn't a religious man by any stretch of the imagination, but if there was a God, I wanted him to find a way to stop this marathon. Maybe a hurricane? An earthquake? A tsunami perhaps?

Then all of a sudden, Jackson Edwards emerged from the crowd and ran toward the starting line like a bat out of hell. He pushed people out of the way, waving, a gun in his hands. The cops were chasing him, their guns also held high and ready. Cameron saw him and bravely pushed Jackson. The crowd hushed.

Jackson didn't even hesitate. He shot Cameron in the right kneecap. People started running toward their cars. Others ducked for fear of more gunfire. Ally hid behind me. Cameron grabbed his knee and went down in pain.

Jackson took off, running wildly. The police caught up to him and tackled him to the ground.

I looked up at the sky. I guess there was actually a God. Guess I did do the right thing in saving Jackson.

***

Ally and I visited Cameron in the hospital. There were reporters in every corner of the white hospital room. His entire right leg was in a cast and was already covered with ink, smiley faces, and "get well soon" sayings.

He looked at us and smiled. "Hey, guys!"

"Hi Cameron," I said.

"How are you feeling?" Ally asked.

"The doctors said that I can't run. Damn bastard broke my kneecap in several places."

"That really sucks," I said and nodded sympathetically. "You were going to raise so much money, too. I mean, wow, those whales could have used it, too."

Cameron nodded. "I let them down, that's for sure. I let you down, too, Arran."

I laughed inside. "It's all right, Cameron. Next year, you can run the marathon again and I'll make sure to put in some money per mile."

"A thousand per mile?" Cameron asked.

I thought about it. "Well, the economy's not supposed to be that great next year. Maybe like a hundred per mile. Per mile," I said, putting a strong emphasis on 'per mile.'

"Arran, can I ask you a question?"

"Technically, you already asked me a question, but go ahead."

"Remember the other day at Blockbuster, you were going to offer me five thousand up front?"

Shit, seriously? He actually remembered? "Of course, what about it?"

"I would like to take you up on that offer, if you don't mind."

I looked around the room. Cameras were everywhere. Reporters held microphones inches from my face. I didn't have much of a choice. I looked at Ally. "Sure," I replied. "Five thousand."

"You're the best, Arran" he replied. He looked at all of the reporters. "You guys should all appreciate what this man has done. He's a special man. A very special man."

I felt my face grow hot. Anger swirled through me. "Not a problem. Anything for you," I spat.

Cameron winked into the camera. "I probably should have taken you up on your offer anyways. I mean, I was struggling to even reach two miles."

"But you said you were at fifteen miles," Arran said.

"I know, and I'm sorry that I lied to you. You cared so much about saving the whales, I didn't want to disappoint you."

My stomach dropped. I should have known. Bastard. "Can I sign your cast?" I asked, smiley brightly.

"Absolutely!" Cameron beamed.

Ally handed me a pen. I found a blank spot on the cast. "To Cameron," I wrote, "here is your $5,000 dollars. Take it and shove it up your ass."

I signed my name with force, with pride, and smiled into a camera lens as I left the room.

The Song Remains the Same in Your Head

"Music and rhythm find their way into the secret places of the soul."
Plato

Gregory Hill was walking in downtown Bend, Oregon, thinking of his big date in a couple of hours. He'd finally gotten the nerve to ask the lovely Meredith Moser, a security analyst at Wells Fargo, for a date. To his astonishment, she accepted and had seemed quite delighted at the prospect.

It was a beautiful day in Bend. The sun was shining. Gregory had a skip to his step. As he walked down Main Street looking for a shop in which to pick up a new shirt for his date, a melody kept knocking at his consciousness.

Where the hell did that come from? he wondered.

Then he thought of the radio show he listened to as he drove into town. The deejay had talked about some of his favorite cartoons from his childhood. Among his top five was *Chip 'N Dale Rescue Rangers,* a popular Saturday morning Disney cartoon from the late 80s and early 90s.

Gregory watched that show every week when he was a kid. And now, he had the theme song stuck in his head.

Unable to resist, he began whistling the song as he walked past the Tower Theatre. Soon, he started to sing.

> *Some times, some crimes*
> *Go slippin' through the cracks*

An older man wearing a Hawaiian shirt crossed his path, then stopped in his tracks. He joined Gregory in the tune.

> *But these two, gumshoes*
> *Are pickin' up the slack*

They sang together and enticed a couple of women who'd been window-shopping to join in.

> *There's no case too big, no case too small*
> *When you need help just call*

The volume increased with each added voice and soon, everyone on the street was clutching each other's arms and singing along.

Ch-ch-ch-Chip 'N Dale, Rescue Rangers
Ch-ch-ch-Chip 'N Dale, when there's danger!

Gregory stepped forward to take on a solo.

Oh no it never fails, once they're involved
Somehow whatever's wrong gets solved!

Everyone in downtown Bend joined in the fun.

Ch-ch-ch-Chip 'N Dale, Rescue Rangers
Ch-ch-ch-Chip 'N Dale, when there's danger.

Gregory spread his arms wide as he belted out another solo.

Oh no it never fails …

Gregory's eyes widened and his lips remained parted, but no words came out. He'd suddenly developed a brain cramp. His lips moved idly as he hummed the rest of the song, trying to figure out what the lyrics were. He looked around at the crowd of people and saw only blank faces. No one could recall those words.

Oh no it never fails …

Gregory sang again, thinking it would jump start his brain. But it didn't. After a few awkward moments, everyone returned to what they'd been doing before the song had taken over the street.

"Fuck," Gregory muttered. Now this was going to bother him all day long. "Does anyone know the *Rescue Rangers* theme song?" he cried out. "Does anyone know the theme song to *Chip 'N Dale Rescue Rangers*? Anyone?"

No one responded. He ran up to a businesswoman who held one of those new zPhones in her hands.

"Excuse me, ma'am, could you look up some lyrics for me?" Gregory asked.

"Get lost," she snapped and walked away.

Gregory darted to a man with a zPhone and rushed over to him. "Excuse me, sir, can I use the Internet on your phone?" The man turned and walked on.

Gregory's head was about to explode. He didn't know the rest of the song. He stood at the corner like a lost puppy. The bus stopped in front of him and he got on, hoping to find an answer. "Anyone here know the lyrics to *Chip 'N Dale Rescue Rangers*?" he shouted.

There was a long, silent pause.

And then, like music to his ears, someone from the back shouted, "Yeah, I do."

Gregory ran to the back, knocking into people's elbows and feet. When he reached the back, a man with a knotted brown beard nodded. Panting and out of breath he said, "You know the theme song?" Gregory asked.

"Yeah, totally man." He cleared his throat and sang.

Life is like a hurricane here in Duckburg.
Race cars, lasers, aeroplanes, it's a ...

"No, no, no! That's *Ducktales*!" Gregory exclaimed. "Rescue Rangers! *Some times, some crimes. Go slippin' through the cracks!*"

"What the fuck is that?" the man asked.

"*Rescue Rangers!*"

"*Rescue Rangers*? Sounds gay."

"It's not gay. How can a song be gay?" Gregory shook his head and yelled, "Anyone know the theme song to *Rescue Rangers*?"

"Sir, will you please sit down and be quiet?" the bus driver called out over the loudspeaker.

Gregory returned to his seat and glanced at the man who was humming the *DuckTales* theme song.

***

Gregory got off the bus at the next stop and headed toward the library. He would use one of the computers to find the lyrics.

When he walked in, all the computers were taken. *Shit*. But as if on cue, a man got up and left his computer. Gregory raced to take the still-warm seat.

His fingers found their rightful place on the keyboard, and he was about to type out the name of the show, when he looked up at the screen and was shocked by the image. The computer had been left on a pornography site featuring hot milfs performing sexual acts on horses.

Before Gregory could collect his senses and click off the site, an older woman walked by and glanced at the screen.

"What are you looking at?" she complained in a loud and outraged voice.

Gregory looked at her. "This isn't what you think!"

"It looks like they are having sex with horses."

Gregory looked at the screen. "Well, yes, but I wasn't the one searching this site. It was the guy before me."

"You're one sick bastard," she said in a shrill scream. She turned and addressed the quiet and studious people by shouting hysterically, "This man is looking at horse porn! Horse porn!"

Everyone turned to glance at the perversion on Gregory's screen. One by one, they looked at him with a combination of shock and dismay, though one guy seemed strangely curious and even winked at him.

"This is a huge misunderstanding!"

An old woman who worked at the library walked up to Gregory. "Sir, I'm going to have to ask you to leave."

"You don't get it. I was going to look for the lyrics to *Rescue Rangers*!"

"That is the biggest bunch of baloney I've ever heard," the old woman said.

"I was! Please don't kick me out! I just need to know …"

"Sir, please leave the library before I call the police."

"Sick bastard!" one of the library patrons shouted.

"I wasn't looking at horse porn!" Gregory said as he got up. "I don't even like looking at horse porn! I'm more into the girl-on-girl. Anyway, I'm not a horse person. I'm barely a porn person. But I'm really big into Disney cartoons and I need to get the lyrics …"

"Shut up!" the old woman snapped. She leaned over and changed the page on the screen so none of the children could see the strange and bizarre images. "If I ever see you in this library again, I will call the police and have you arrested."

The library couldn't get any quieter. All eyes bore on Gregory.

He stood and asked one more question. "Any of you know the theme song to *Rescue Rangers*?"

An adorable little red-haired girl put her hand in the air and began to sing. "*Oh no it never fails ...*"

"Sush, Lexi." The girl's mother quickly stepped in and swept the child into her arms. "You never, ever want to talk to this man."

"Go on," he begged of the little girl.

"Get out!" everyone yelled in unison.

Gregory ran out of the library frustrated, but still intent on finding the missing lyrics. He looked at his watch. It was almost time for his date. *Maybe Meredith would know the lyrics.*

***

Gregory sat at a corner table at the Pine Tavern with Meredith. Stunning in a fabulously sexy red dress and daring red heels, Meredith was a vision of beauty. Her red lips, blonde hair and never-ending legs were all Gregory had thought about for the past month. But now...

"So, how was your day?" Meredith asked.

"*Oh no it never fails ...*" Gregory sang under his breath.

Meredith frowned. "What did you say?"

Gregory looked at her. "Oh, sorry. I'm just trying to remember the rest of this song that's been stuck in my head."

"What song?" She seemed mildly interested and possibly eager to help.

"The *Chip 'N Dale Rescue Rangers* theme song."

"Is that a cartoon?" Her head tilted curiously to one side.

"Oh, yeah. You must have heard it a thousand times. It played on TV every week. Remember? Everyone's heard it."

"I don't think I watched ..."

"Oh, how could you have not?" he asked with ill-concealed irritation.

"Well, maybe I saw it a few times, but I don't really remember it."

"Oh, you have to! You must! Chip and Dale were two chipmunks who solved cases."

Meredith shook her blonde little head.

"Do you remember Monterey Jack? He loved cheese like it was crack? Remember Zipper the fly? Actually, he was kind of freaky. I mean, he was like half the size of a chipmunk. And he was strong as …"

"I've never heard of that show," Meredith confessed, interrupting Gregory. "I was more of a *DuckTales* person myself."

"But it came on right after *DuckTales*. Surely you stuck around to at least watch the opening and hear …"

Meredith shook her head and her jaw tightened slightly. "Can we change the subject?"

"Sure, sure," Gregory said. "So, what do you like to do for fun?" she asked.

"I like to read, watch movies, play sports…" He tapped his foot obnoxiously. He couldn't stop fidgeting. What were those damn lyrics? "I find it surprising that someone who watched *DuckTales* doesn't know about Rescue Rangers? I mean, what was so important that you got up and left right after *DuckTales*. It's inconceivable. Are you sure you …"

Meredith took a sip of wine, set her glass down with ladylike calm, then angrily stood. "I don't know what your obsession with some old cartoon is, but I think I've had quite enough. I spent a hundred bucks on this dress, two-fucking-hundred on the shoes, and I spent an hour getting ready. And for what? A fucking discussion about silly kiddie cartoons? I'm sorry, but this is just too weird for me. I have no clue what your problem is, but I'm going to leave now! Have a nice night."

Gregory didn't bother trying to stop her as she walked away from the table and strutted outside. His face lit up and his lips spread in a satisfied smile. "I have no clue," he murmured. "I have no clue … clue!" And the melody started up again.

*Oh no it never fails, they'll take the clues
And find the wheres and whys and whos!*

A few heads turned to him and sang along. People seated further away soon joined in. Soon, everyone in the restaurant was singing the *Rescue Rangers* song.

> *Ch-ch-ch-Chip 'N Dale, Rescue Rangers*
> *Ch-ch-ch-Chip 'N Dale, when there's danger!*
> *Ch-ch-ch-Chip 'N Dale!*

When the explosive rendition of the song came to an end, everyone applauded. Gregory nodded, bowed, and smiled at the crowd. He was so excited. He finally found the answer. As he went to take a sip of wine and thank Meredith, she was already gone.

He threw a few bills on the table, ran out of the restaurant, and spotted her heading east. "Meredith!" he cried out as he hurried to catch her.

"Leave me alone."

"I wanted to thank you for getting that song out of my head."

"Well, isn't that nice. I'm glad I could help get that *Captain Planet* song out of your head. God, I've never met a stranger person than you!" She quickened her pace to a trot.

"It was *Rescue Rangers*, not *Captain Planet*!" he replied and he followed her.

And then he stopped.. He got a new song stuck in his head. He sang out.

> *Captain Planet, he's our hero*
> *Gonna take pollution down to zero*
> *He's our powers magnified*
> *And he's ...*

And he's ... He's ... He's what?

> *He's our powers magnified*
> *And he's ...*

Damn it. Not again.

Watch for Little Brother

"We are rapidly entering the age of no privacy, where everyone is open to surveillance at all times; where there are no government secrets."

William Orville Douglas

Rebekah Stein sat at the receptionist desk of the psychiatric hospital in Eugene observing the surveillance camera across the lobby. She really hated that camera. She knew it was supposed to be watching the doors, but she was positive that her boss had turned the camera to make sure she was doing her job and not falling asleep. Sometimes, she would just sit and stare at the camera. She even flipped the camera the bird just to see if her boss noticed.

A male patient walked up to her desk. His hair was a messy brown mop. His opened robe exposed his pasty-white hairless chest. "Excuse me," he said to Rebekah.

She didn't pay attention to him. She barely heard him. She was mesmerized by the camera.

"Excuse me!" he said again, loudly.

Rebekah snapped out of it and looked at him. "What? What is it?"

"Ummm … are you okay?" he asked.

"Yes, I'm fine," she said, keeping one eye on the camera.

The man looked quite perplexed. "Can you tell me where the bathroom is?"

"Yeah, it's right through there," she said, pointing at the exit. She couldn't care less about the man; she was focused on that damn camera.

"Ummm … where's there?"

"Out there," she replied. She wished he would just leave her alone.

"Okay … when I get out there, where do I go?"

Rebekah stared at him angrily. "There will be signs to the bathroom when you get out there. Just follow them, okay?"

The patient shook his head and grumbled as he walked away.

It's about bloody time, she thought. She continued to stare at the camera. She hated her boss but she hated being watched more. Her boss was the type of man who thought he was suave. Wore pinstriped pants with colorful buttoned-down shirts and penny loafers. Never referred to Rebekah by her name, only "my assistant." Got his teeth bleached every six months. What was worse, he never complimented her on a job well done. She came in on weekends, answered his beckoning calls, and never once received a thank you. Instead, she had to deal with crazy-ass patients, even crazier family members, and a camera.

She once threw a clipboard at the camera from her desk, but missed and made a dent in the ceiling. She had enough. She thought he should trust her to do her job without constantly peeking in on her, playing God, and watching her every move. It really bothered her. She was a big girl; she didn't need to be treated like a small kid. She didn't want to be controlled by anyone … she just wanted to be herself. And that camera was preventing her from doing so.

With no one in the lobby, she grabbed the fire extinguisher from underneath her desk and walked toward the camera. She looked up and stared at its red light, trying to plot out her next move. The weight of the fire extinguisher already tired her, so she set it down to find some way of reaching the camera. She grabbed a chair, pushed it under the camera, and tried to turn it off, but she couldn't reach it. She ran to the waiting area and picked up a couple of phone books and magazines, set them on top of the chair, and reached up again. Still, no luck.

She looked at the line of chairs. They should stack up nicely, she decided. She kicked a few over to the chair already in place, then balanced one on top of the other. She climbed on one chair, then teetered back to set the fire extinguisher on the second chair before stepping up. The camera was almost within reach. She could almost see into its nosy, beady little insides.

Holding her breath and drooling with anticipation, she climbed up the third chair.

And there it was. Smack in her face. She hit the camera with the fire extinguisher. The lens cracked and the thin metallic side dented. She chuckled and snickered and was soon laughing hysterically.

By the time Rebekah realized, it was too late. She was losing her balance and she struggled to find something to grasp. In desperation, she let the extinguisher fall to the tiled floor and hugged the chair in front of her. Lightweight and useless, it didn't help, and she fell, bringing the chair clattering to the floor with her. Before her back could register an ounce of pain, her head made a firm and solid contact with the floor. She looked up to see the second chair fall onto her.

She'd done it! She destroyed that mother-fucking camera. It couldn't bother her anymore. She was free from the tyranny of her boss. She was free from anyone watching her! She had the freedom to do whatever she damned well pleased. *Look out world, here I come!*

But then, as she tried to move, Rebekah realized that her body felt numb. She couldn't feel her feet. Her head pounded. She slowly pushed the chair off her stomach and reached behind her head. Her fingers felt something sticky on the floor. Blood? Had she cracked her head open? She felt woozy. She tried to move, but couldn't.

Would someone please help her?

Was there anyone watching her?

As she closed her eyes, the camera's glaring red light faded to black.

Mother Nature can Kiss MY ASS

"Human beings, as a species, have no more value than slugs."

John Davis

My wife Stephanie and I were seated at the back of the auditorium of Lewis and Clark College, watching a presentation by crazy environmentalist Forest Williams. I highly doubted Forest was his birth name. It was probably something like Dale or Gary or Frankie. Anyway, I was dragged to this presentation from hell because my wife had read a book by this nutcase. Stephanie was not an environmentalist, but I think she was in the process of becoming a convert.

Forest stood behind the podium with a bright and unbelievably ugly bowtie that would make Congressman Earl Blumenauer puke.

"We must protect the earth for a number of reasons," he said. "First off, ethically, most people have a unique bond with nature and many, like myself, feel it is our duty to preserve it. Secondly, we need to preserve our own species. Protecting the environment protects animals, and in turn, protecting animals protects us. We rely on the ecosystem to live. We eat plants, use the wood from trees, and countless other plants for medications and the like. Humans are, indeed, at risk."

I was starting to fall asleep. *Blah, blah, blah, blah.* God, and I was missing coverage of the NBA Draft for this? Portland had the fifth pick in the draft!

"All in all, we must protect our environment from destruction, to prevent our *own* destruction," said Forest.

The crowd applauded and my torture was over.

***

In the weeks that followed, Stephanie didn't miss a chance to remind me of our environmental responsibilities.

One fine evening, I popped open a can of beer, settled into my favorite chair, and planned on watching a few hours of TV.

Stephanie walked into the room, her eyes scanning for any environmental transgression. And it didn't take her long. She noticed the nice pile of newspapers next to me.

"Josh, are you going to recycle those newspapers?" she asked.

I dragged my eyes away from the tube and looked at her. Her long, dark hair hung loosely down her back and she was wearing those hip-hugging jeans and a fabulously revealing top. Johnny boy jumped to attention and made my jeans suddenly tight and uncomfortable. I gazed at her with my best bedroom eyes, but seeing the look on her face, I knew there was no point getting excited. "Recycle?"

She rolled her eyes. "Didn't you learn anything from Forest?"

I tried to remain focused, but my gaze repeatedly returned to the opening in her shirt. Damn it, why did she do that? How could she flash her breasts at me like that while nagging me about a stupid pile of newspapers? "I learned just how much of a douche he was."

She rolled her eyes again. "Recycling is very important. You do realize recycling helps to reduce the pollution caused by waste, don't you? Recycling paper takes half the energy needed to produce new paper. Most trash consists of paper in one form or another. Every hundred pounds of trash contains thirty-five pounds of paper ..."

Blah, blah, blah. The tedium of that lecture lived on in the form of my pretty little wife. God, I couldn't believe she'd turned into Forest. She'd gone completely green and shit.

"The benefits of recycling paper are endless; less waste in landfills, less pollution in the environment from the manufacturing processes and less disruption to nature. Do you understand?"

"Yes, I do."

"What did I just say?" She firmly set her fists on her hips, cocked her head to one side, and looked expectantly at me.

Damn, was I going to have to recite the whole pathetic lecture? "You said recycling paper is good."

"Good. I'm hitting the shower." She unbuttoned her shirt, revealing the sexiest lilac bra I'd ever seen. It had lacy little flowers bordering the edge and working its way up the straps where a series of small, green leaves covered...

Green leaves? No. I couldn't take anymore green!

"Make sure those newspapers are in the recycling bin."

"We have a recycling bin?"

"Now we do." She smiled and peeled off her shirt.

Damn.

She headed for the stairs and I watched every step. Good grief, I needed another beer. I couldn't believe that psycho environmentalist had successfully converted my wife into a green goblin.

I walked into the kitchen to grab a cool beer and a couple of ice cubes. Stephanie bought cups that were 100% biodegradable, recyclable, special paper carbon, whatever. I took one of these special cups, filled it with delicious beer, and then dropped the ice cubes in.

I adjusted my crotch, and considered heading upstairs to join Stephanie. With one foot on the first step, I heard her singing…

"Pave paradise, put up a parking …"

Shit. I returned to the living room and stretched out on the couch. Flipping through the channels, I came to the weather report. God weathermen sucked.

"Today's temperature is two degrees hotter than it was yesterday!"

Thank you, mister obvious! I could have figured that out by opening a window. And why did they insist on telling me about weather that was thousands of miles away in an area I didn't live in? I was in Oregon, not Ohio.

Suddenly, I felt something cold and wet on my stomach. I looked at my cup of beer and noticed that golden liquid was dripping out of my cup and onto my Portland Winter Hawks shirt. Mother fucking cup! I put the cup down on the floor and got up to clean myself. This was my favorite shirt! Son of a bitch! I pulled the shirt over my head and went to the kitchen sink to rinse it out. As much as I loved beer, the stale old smell of beer on my clothes was downright gross. I wasn't in college anymore.

Bitter and angry, I muttered curses to that damned environmentalist as I turned on the faucet and let gallons of fresh, pure water pour over my beloved shirt.

Forest's blasphemous rhetoric and propaganda regarding recycling and the environment was making me nauseous and pissed. This whole state was turning green because of this hippie bastard who probably drove around in a big fucking SUV when no one was looking. I bet the hypocrite didn't even turn off the water when he brushed his teeth. At least *I* did that. Only I didn't go around touting myself as some green, ecological, all-knowing wizard who preached how to do the right thing.

Forest tried to scare us by saying that we had less than ten years to fix our crazy level of pollution or we'd head straight to some super catastrophic bye-bye Earth death. According to him, we needed to start driving more hybrids, stop driving cars with testicles, find alternative (read: shitty) sources of energy, and come up with crappier, greener versions of literally everything. If he had his way, we'd all be forced to use greener masturbation techniques like using the same magazine again and again, and then recycling it once you've soiled all the pages, even the ads. Better yet, draw your own jerk-off material on the back of a used napkin, then use the napkin to clean up after yourself when you were done.

I had to do something about this!

After dumping the pile of newspapers in the trash, I spent all night devising a plan to seek my revenge against Forest and his green movement. I took out a notepad and a pen. Even before I had opened the pad or written anything down, I noticed the words printed at the bottom of the cover: *Made from Recycled Paper.* I crumbled each piece of recycled shit and tossed it in the trash. With every piece of paper I tore, I felt as though I was ripping apart each and every one of Forest's bloody organs. That was when it hit me. I knew what I had to do.

***

The next morning, I got up early, got into my H3 Hummer, and drove to the local Fred Meyer. I bought several gas cans, quarts of motor oil, bags of fertilizer, a chainsaw, and all the foam cups they had in stock. Then, I drove to the local dump where I collected as many bags of filthy, stinking garbage as I possibly could.

I then drove to Oswego Lake, a beautiful place where the water was crystal clear. Some said that it was one of the few unspoiled pieces of nature in Oregon. I pulled the SUV right up to the lake and dumped all of my crap in and around the water.

I laughed with glee. Take that, Forest!

After that, I took out the trash and all the Styrofoam in my car and set it all on fire. The black smoke billowed into the morning sky. I was laughing like a fucking hyena.

High on this rush of polluting power, I took out my chainsaw and started cutting down the trees around the lake. I managed to topple one of the larger Aspens or Firs or whatever fucking tree it was, and watched with satisfaction as a domino effect wiped out a total of eleven other trees. By the time I was done, the shoreline looked like a hurricane had devastated the area.

Avenged and proud, I got in my Hummer and took the dirt road back to the main highway. A stupid little baby deer had the nerve to step out into my path and look at me with those big sad eyes. Did it really think I cared? I hit the gas and ran straight into the sucker as the mother stood on the edge of the forest watching. I was on a roll, unstoppable.

I headed to the local department store and bought as many over-packaged, chemically-ridden products as I could. Damn hypocrites.

When I got to the cashier, she asked if I had my environmentally-friendly shopping bags.

I glared at her and shook my head.

"Well, then," she said as she threw her snotty green nose in the air. "I'll have to charge you five cents per bag."

I cocked a brow and held her gaze. Did she really think she was scaring me with these financial tactics? Was five cents really supposed to deter me from using the convenient plastic bags from the store?

Well, hell, I had something to teach her, to teach all of them. I glanced at a number of the shopping carts behind me. All were filled with a variety of environmentally unfriendly junk. And finally, in the third cart back, I saw what I wanted. I squeezed past the other carts, the shoppers eyeing me with wide and curious eyes. I reached into that third cart and looked at the young woman pushing it. "May I?" I asked.

She nodded.

I returned to the cashier and plunked down a box of *Happy Sturdy Garbage Bags*. "You see this?" I asked.

She looked at the box as though not understanding, but I knew she knew where I was going with this.

But for the benefit of all those behind me and the cashiers nearby, I made my point loud and clear. "These strong, resistant bags will break down in a million years because of the poly-urethane or whatever shit they are made of."

"Yes, sir, and they're our best selling brand. They even control garbage odor and …"

"I'm throwing the shit away. I'm not keeping garbage as a memento!"

"It keeps your kitchen smelling fresh and …"

"For the past twelve years I've been using bags from here and the grocery store. Not only were they free, but I thought they did a mighty fine job, and hell, I already had them so, why not?" I grabbed a fistful of shopping bags from the rack in front of her. "I mean, why should I throw this away…" I picked up the box of garbage bags. "In these?"

"Well, those are more resistant and …"

"I'm not throwing away a fucking piano in these bags. All I throw away is food and the excess package of all the junk *you guys* sell!"

The crowd behind me started to get agitated. I could feel they were moving to my side.

"And you want me to feel bad because you're going to charge me five fucking cents for one of these." I held up the shopping bags. "Well, look at this." I shoved the box of garbage bags in her face.

"What?" she asked with an idiotic expression on her face.

"This costs almost five bucks for forty-eight bags."

Everyone was listening.

"That's ten cents per bag. And it'll probably sit in a landfill a hell of a lot longer than this." I popped open a store shopping bag and held it up for everyone to see. "The way I see it, I'm five cents ahead."

The crowd was amazed by this revelation and several reached into their carts to pull out their boxes of *Happy Sturdy Garbage Bags*.

I smiled at the cashier. "I'll take ten of those bags, if you don't mind."

My day's work was done and I headed home.

***

I opened the door to the house and called out for Stephanie. When no answer came, I went to the kitchen for a refreshing beer, straight from the can, thank you. I was about to jump into my recliner when I saw the message machine blinking.

"Hi, honey, it's me. Me, Rachel, and Georgina are heading out to Oswego Lake with Branson and Thomas. Would be great if you could join us. See you later."

Hmmm.

Second message. "Honey? It's me again. I'm not feeling too well and neither is Georgina. Thomas is going to take us to Emanuel Hospital."

Within ten minutes, I was at the hospital.

Before I entered her room, Dr. Reese informed me of her condition. "She appears to have ingested some very toxic chemicals. The labs just came back with the results of the water we got from her hair and we found alarming amounts of petroleum products. This has caused some serious bacterial infections and there's the possibility of brain damage."

I thanked the doctor and entered Stephanie's room. She looked like crap. Her face was almost green. How strangely appropriate.

"Oh, honey," she said with a weak smile. "I'm so happy you came."

"You're going to be fine," I told her as I reached for her hand. It was still slick from the oil. I felt my stomach churn. I had done this to her. I didn't know what to think.

"I just don't understand. Who would pour motor oil into that beautiful lake?" she asked.

Suddenly, Forest sauntered into the room all smiles and whistles carrying a huge bundle of roses. Stephanie's eyes lit up when she saw him and her smile was brighter than I'd ever seen.

"How are you feeling?" Forest asked as he walked around to the opposite side of the bed and handed her the roses.

"You didn't have to bring me roses!" she replied. He leaned over to hug her and give her a peck on her forest green cheek. Ugh … a sore sight for good eyes.

"I thought I had to make up for this horrible mess. See what happens when someone ruins the environment? It hurts everyone."

Was he giving a green speech while my wife lay in a hospital bed? God, this guy pissed me off. I couldn't stop my hands from shaking. I really wanted to stick a recycled metal pole up his green ass.

"That's what I was telling my husband," Stephanie told him.

Forest looked at me as he took a hold of my wife's hand. Was that a challenge I saw in his eyes? I tightened my hold on Stephanie's hand.

"You have such a strong wife. You're really very lucky." He brought her motor-oiled hand to his lips.

Good Lord. Was he trying to start an affair with her. I had to get this guy out of the room.

I saw some cups on a table. I grabbed two and went out into the hall where the coffee machine was. I filled my cup with cold water and filled his cup with some hot, hot coffee. Like the true gentleman that I was, I handed the cup of coffee to Forest.

"Want some coffee, Forest?"

"Thanks." He looked at the cup with pride. "Completely bio-degradable. They're made by *Green Go I,* a company that specializes in producing a variety of items from corn, potatoes and beets. I'm the one who introduced these to the hospital a few weeks ago. The cafeteria also uses forks, spoons, and knives made from potatoes." He took a sip from the cup.

I smiled. It wouldn't be long.

"Ah! What is this?"

And there it was. Steaming hot coffee seeped out of the cup and trickled down his hand and onto his white, environmentally-grown cotton shirt. He dropped the cup and coffee splashed all over the floor.

"Son of a bitch!" Forest exclaimed. He looked at his burned, red hand. His face turned a crimson red color. "That coffee just burned right through the cup."

I looked at his hand. "Weak cup, I guess."

"Apparently so," Forest replied. "Are those the same cups I recommended?"

I held up my dripping cup of cold water and looked underneath it. "Yep. *Green Go I* is stamped right there," I cheerfully said. "It's 100% bio-degradable, just like you said, and made from corn."

"But I ... the manufacturers told me that ..." Forest looked at his red hand then at the cup on the floor. "You sure?"

"Uh huh," I reassured him.

Forest looked at his burned hand again. "I can't believe the cups could prove so inadequate. Look at my hand!" he cried out. "Nurse! Nurse," he called as he walked out of the room. "Somebody help me."

Stephanie stared at me. "What the hell was that all about?" she asked.

"I don't know." I squeezed her hand. "I think all this green stuff is driving him a bit crazy."

"I'll say," she replied. She looked at the roses. that were still on her. "Can you take care of these roses? They're scratching me to death."

"Sure. Want me to put them in the compost bin?"

"Nah. Throw them in the trash."

I smiled.

second chance

"If you have made mistakes, even serious ones, there is always another chance for you. What we call failure is not the falling down but the staying down."

Mary Pickford

It was another beautiful summer day in the great city of Portland. The sun was out, the birds were chirping and, more importantly, the people were out in full force. This was going to be a perfect day. I walked up to an older man standing next to the entrance of the Pioneer Place shopping mall. He had a map opened up in front of him and was turning it as he looked at the street sign, then back at the map, trying to figure out where he was.

"Hi there," I said.

"Hi," he replied. "Can you help me out?"

"Sure."

"I'm looking for Powell's Books."

"Oh, of course. Well, you just keep going down 4th, then make a left on Burnside. You can't miss it."

He smiled. "Thanks. You Oregonians are so nice."

"You're welcome. Have a great day."

I walked away with not only a smile on my face, but with the man's wallet in my pocket. I opened the wallet and found a couple hundred dollars and three different credit cards. I never understood why people needed so many cards, but oh well. So far, I'd stolen three wallets, collected seven credit cards, and raked in over five hundred dollars in cash. I decided to celebrate by dining at the Portland City Grill.

On the way to my celebration, I spotted another man. He looked dazed and lost, his eyes darting every which way as though searching for something. This was going to be too easy.

"Are you lost?" I asked.

"Yeah, I'm looking for the Portland Classical Chinese Gardens. I thought it was around here." He adjusted his glasses and peered down the street.

"You're very close. Just walk up to Everett and take a left. You can't miss it."

"Oh, yeah. That's right. Everett. Thanks."

"Not a problem, kind sir. Have a nice day and enjoy the sun."

"Oh, I will! I always thought it rained all the time here in Portland. God, you guys have the best summers."

"Hidden secret," I replied with a smile the welcome wagon would be proud of.

The man walked away, happy as could be. And the secret, Mr. Chinese Gardens— I just took your wallet. A hundred dollars, a couple of credit cards, and huh? A police badge from Seattle? I fingered the shiny badge and looked at the name. Officer Bransford. How interesting. Well, I knew what I was going to dress up as on Halloween.

I turned to head for the Portland City Grill and walked straight to a window table. I ordered a great bottle of wine and a terrific four-course meal. I even offered this hot chick a glass of my unbelievably expensive Pinot Noir. She, in turn, gave me her number. I made a private toast to Officer Bransford, thanking him for the money.

I walked out feeling full and a tad tipsy. I looked up at the darkening sky and wondered where the brilliant noonday sun had gone. Man, it was dark. I shrugged and figured I'd probably enjoyed myself longer than I'd thought.

On the way back to my car, I cut through a small alley. I was about to step out of the alley and take the main street to my car when I saw Officer Bransford.

Shit. I stopped and held my breath. Had he yet noticed his missing identity? Would he remember talking to me?

But, luckily, he didn't even notice me passing by. He was too busy helping a young girl who had fallen down.

"Let me help you up, sweetheart," he said as he took a hold of her arm and guided her to her feet.

Suddenly, a mad woman came running out from a nearby shop and attacked him.

"What are you doing?" she screamed, as she repeatedly struck him with an impressively large purse. "Get your hands off my daughter!"

"Miss. Miss, please," he said as he brought his arms up to protect his face. "Your daughter just fell down. I was helping her up."

"You touched my daughter!" she cried out. "You laid your filthy, old man hands on my little girl."

"Ma'am, she wanted my help." Bransford stepped out of range of her swinging purse. "Look at her knee. She's all scraped up. I was just ..."

"I'm calling the police!"

"I'm a police officer," he replied.

"Yeah, right."

"Ma'am, I'm Officer Bransford."

"Really? Then show me your badge." She looked defiantly at him and waited.

Bransford searched through his pockets for his wallet. "Hmmm." He began the process again, carefully patting every pocket. "Where's my wallet?" he muttered to himself. "I had it here earlier. I had it when I…"

"Show me your badge!" she yelled. "You filthy animal. You're not an officer!"

"I have it somewhere." His hands continued the search. "I took it out to pay for…"

"Help!" she cried out, as she grabbed a hold of her daughter. "Help!"

A couple of young men heard the cry and came running toward the mother. They each grabbed a baseball bat from a discount bin in front of a sporting goods store.

"He touched my daughter!" she screamed. "This pervert touched my precious little girl."

"I'm a police officer!" Bransford tried to explain. "I wouldn't harm her! I'm an officer of the law."

Bransford suddenly saw me and his eyes widened in surprise, then narrowed in accusation. "You!" he yelled at me. "You … stop right there!"

He ran toward me.

Shit.

Before I could think to run away, the bat-wielding men took care of him. One of them hit the officer behind the knees, while the other swung for the back.

Bransford fell down with a groan and a thud. They beat him relentlessly. Blood splattered everywhere, and onlookers stood frozen watching the scene. Nobody helped. Bransford soon stopped fighting back and lay limp on the concrete.

I wanted to run and help him, but I couldn't. I was frozen and felt helpless. One of the men gave a final kick to assure he was dead. The men scurried from the scene. The woman held her daughter's face to her bosom muttering under her breath, "The pig deserved it. Now he'll never bother another young, innocent girl again."

Jesus Christ. I couldn't believe what I'd just witnessed.

I walked up to Bransford, lying dead in an immense pool of his own blood. That was when it hit me: I'd killed him. I'd stolen his wallet and his life. He could have gone after me and taken me down. But those guys nailed him in the back. God had given me a second chance to realize what I had done.

I took out his wallet and threw it on his stomach. It was time to start my life anew. Of course, I took a twenty from him before I left.

Finder's fee, you know.

our only Hope

"On the whole, human beings want to be good, but not too good, and not quite all the time."

George Orwell

It was Tuesday in Forest Grove. David Fowble slouched in his armchair, watching the Portland Trail Blazers take on the LA Lakers. With his Dead Guy Ale in one hand and his TV controller in the other, he was ready to cheer on his team. Then, the phone rang.

His wife, Misty, answered it from the kitchen and then called out, "David!"

"What?"

"It's the Lord of Darkness. Want to answer it?"

David sighed. He was the Human Representative for the Council of the Lords. *Why did I join that council anyway?* he thought. "What does he want?" David asked in a whiny tone.

"I don't know, but he says it's very important."

"Fine, give me the phone," David replied.

She walked into the living room and tossed him the phone. He lowered the volume on the TV and put the phone to his ear. "This is David."

"This is the Lord of Darkness," a low, powerful voice said.

"Yeah, Lord, can you make this quick? This game is about to start. Blazers and Lakers; playoffs are on the line."

"I am very unhappy."

"So am I," David replied.

"Mandatory council meeting right now. Be there!" the Lord of Darkness said, then hung up the phone.

"Shit," David muttered. "Honey, I have to go meet with the Gods." He pushed himself out of his comfy armchair.

"But isn't the next meeting not for a couple of weeks?" Misty asked.

"Yeah, but the stupid Lord of Darkness is calling for a mandatory meeting."

"Well, okay, but be careful." She looked at him with her lazy eye and smiled.

David glanced back at the basketball game on TV. The two teams tipped off, with the Blazers getting the ball.

"How 'bout you watch the game for me and let me know how it goes?"

She gave him a silly *"of course not"* look and returned to the kitchen.

***

After an amazing, mysterious, and magical journey (which, due to legal ramifications, the narrator cannot explain), David walked inside the Hall of the Gods. Marble pillars stood 12 stories high. A statue of Michelangelo's David sat in a huge, granite fountain spurting water. David's New Balance sneakers squeaked on the tiled floor. A couple of the Gods had already arrived and were taking their seats.

David walked up to the Lord of Time. "Hey, Lord," he said, patting him on the back.

"Hey, David," the Lord of Time replied, adjusting his thick, dark glasses. His long, white beard flowed to the floor.

"What the fuck is going on?"

"I have no idea. I think the Lord of Darkness got up on the wrong side of the bed this morning," he replied.

Suddenly, a collective gasp went through the hall as the sunlight disappeared, leaving everyone in pitch-blackness. As the Lord of Darkness took his seat, the sunlight slowly returned. The Lord of Darkness wore a black robe, the hood covering the majority of his face.

The Lord of Power stood up. "Thank you all for being here. Lord of Darkness, you have summoned all of us here. What is your reason?"

The Lord of Darkness stood. "Thank you, Lord of Power. I am disappointed with the human race."

"Look, Lord, I don't know how many times I've had to say this, but we're sorry about Andy Dick. That was our bad," David said.

"It's not just that," the Lord of Darkness said. "I went down to Earth today, you know, just to see how things were coming along. I was shocked. I was amazed at just how awful human beings are."

"Were you hanging out in New Jersey?" David chimed in.

"No, David. I was vacationing at Crater Lake."

"Oh, beautiful place," David said.

"Yes, it was nice. I was amazed at just how blue that water was. My wife took lots of pictures ..." The Lord of Darkness stopped suddenly and shook his head. "I need to get back on topic. Anyways, the humans were awful. They didn't respect us at all. I remember a time when Gods used to be all powerful, all mighty ... we struck fear into the human race. We were loved. Now, humans couldn't care less about us. Hell, they don't even know who we are. How could this have happened? We are Gods!"

"So what do you propose?" the Lord of Time asked.

"Start a marketing campaign?" David asked.

"No," the Lord of Darkness replied. "I have decided to take matters into my own hands. I have hired an independent contractor to tear down that worthless planet and construct a luxury condominium."

"Will it be eco-friendly?" the Lord of Nature asked. Vines swirled around his arms and a wreath of daisies sat on his head.

Hippie bastard, David thought.

"Yes, Lord of Nature, it will adhere to all energy and environmental standards. It will be built with environmentally-friendly materials," the Lord of Darkness replied.

"You can't blow up the Earth!" David exclaimed.

"You humans are worthless," the Lord of Darkness fired back. "Seriously, what's the point of humanity? You guys have done nothing."

"This is stupid," David said as he looked at the Lord of Power. "Lord, he is so out of line!"

The Lord of Power was deep in thought. "Can I get a penthouse?" he asked the Lord of Darkness.

"There's one with your name on it," the Lord of Darkness replied.

"Wait a minute!" David exclaimed to all the Gods. "Can I have a word here?"

The Lord of Power looked at David. "Go ahead."

"I have to represent the human race. After all, that's my job. We humans have done something. We've traveled all over our entire little planet, and now we're out huntin' more! We got ourselves organized into nice, friendly democratic nations, more or less. We got computers that are getting smarter every day and can do our thinking for us. We've killed diseases that used to be unbeatable. Most of all, we even got ourselves the NBA! And we're not done yet! We're not worthless. We're going to do things so amazing that you Gods will appreciate us."

The Lord of Darkness slammed his fists on the table. "Are you done talking?"

"Let's ask the Lord of Time," David said, as he looked at him. "Lord of Time, tell us. What exciting things will humans do in the future?"

The Lord of Time closed his eyes for a moment and then looked at David.

"So, anything exciting?" The Lord of Power asked.

"The humans blow up Earth," The Lord of Time replied.

David was shocked. "What?"

"Yeah, you guys started out pretty good. Found the cure for cancer and created cars that run on water. But then you really fuck it up in the year 2557."

"So there, we should blow up that pathetic planet and build that condominium!" The Lord of Darkness exclaimed.

The Gods all agreed.

Shit, David thought. But then he had an idea. A master plan to save all of humanity. He walked up to the Lord of Time and whispered in his ear. "Lord of Time, can I talk to you for a second, privately?"

***

It was Tuesday in Forest Grove. David Fowble slouched in his armchair, watching the Portland Trail Blazers take on the LA Lakers. With his Dead Guy Ale in one hand and his TV controller in the other, he was ready to cheer on his team. Then, the phone rang.

His wife, Misty, answered it from the kitchen then called out, "David!"

"What?" David cried out.

"It's the Lord of Darkness. Want to answer it?"

David smiled. "Nah, take a message," he replied.

The Flight

"Commitment in the face of conflict produces character."

Unknown

I walked into the airplane at the Portland International Airport runway, suitcase in hand. I put my suitcase in the overhead bin and took my seat next to the aisle. Suddenly, a beautiful woman was standing right next to me.

"I think you're in my seat," she said.

"I'm sorry, I must have the window," I replied. She was gorgeous. Red hair, like fire, green eyes. Slim waist, perky bust. I got a whiff of her flowery perfume. I slid down to the window seat and watched as she placed her bags in the overhead bin. Man, she brought a lot of bags.

She took her seat and looked at me. "I moved your suitcase a little bit. I hope you don't mind."

"Not at all," I replied. Her skin was smooth and perfect, not a flaw, mole, pore visible to the naked eye. "I'm Eliot, by the way."

She smiled. "I'm Traci. Nice to meet you."

"So is Minnesota your final stop?"

"No. I'm changing planes in Minnesota, then heading to Iowa." She fidgeted around in her seat as she tried to get comfortable. She crossed her legs. Her pencil skirt slid up revealing smooth, tight thighs.

"Really? I'm going to Iowa, too."

"Nice. Why are you heading there?"

"Visiting my family and friends. I'm from Armstrong."

Traci stared at me. "Armstrong, Iowa? Are you serious?"

I looked at her in confusion. "I am serious."

"That's where I'm going. I used to live there. I'm visiting my sister who still lives there."

I laughed. "Amazing. That place has a population of under a thousand."

"Small world."

The flight attendant walked up to us. "Would you like something to drink?"

"I'll just have an Orange Crush," I said.

"Vodka tonic, please," Traci said.

"No problem. That will be five dollars," the flight attendant said. Traci opened her large purse and pulled out her wallet. She set the open wallet on the vacant middle seat between her and I and paid the attendant. I glanced at the wallet and noticed a picture of a young boy.

"Is that your son?" I asked.

"No, that's my sister's little boy."

"What a cute kid."

"He's great," she said, as she put away her wallet. "His name's Danny."

"Got it. I don't have any kids. Guess I need to get married first, huh."

"Well, you don't *have* to. My sister's not married and she's doing great."

The flight attendant handed Traci and I our drinks, then walked up to the next row.

"You look familiar," Traci said.

"I used to be in a rock band that performed all the time at the Daultry Bar."

"I went to that bar all the time with my sister! What was the name of the band? Maybe I heard you play."

"Wicked English."

She looked shocked. "No way!"

"You've heard of us?"

"You guys rocked. You guys were, by far, the best band at the bar."

"That's cool."

"That's crazy!" she said with enthusiasm. "Wow ... what's your name again?"

"It's Eliot. But my rocker name was Easy. My bandmates called me that because I had an easy time talking to the ladies after each show."

Traci's smile faded. "Holy shit."

"What?"

"Do you remember one Fourth of July? After Daultry's, a few of us went to a beach house? A couple of you guys ended up staying the night."

"I think I remember that."

"My sister is Angelina Hamilton. You two hooked up that night."

Angelina Hamilton. The name didn't ring a bell. That night was a blur. I remembered the beach house. One of our groupies' parents owned it and we trashed the place. Broken windows, dishes, pottery. Karaoke machine in the living room. Girls dancing topless on the couches and tables. I drank a lot. Shacked it up with some girl in the laundry room. Yes, I remembered. I threw her on top of the washing machine.

Traci turned white, her lips pale. She looked at me. "Oh, my God. You're the father. You're the one who got Angelina pregnant. Danny is your son. I should have known. He has your eyes."

"What? How do you know?" My heart dropped.

"I remember it! You were the only person Angelina had been with. Not to mention the name Easy-E. I could never forget that."

"Holy shit," I said.

"You left Iowa before she could contact you. Of course, she didn't have your number, address, or anything."

"I can't believe this."

"She is going to be so happy to see you."

I looked out the window a moment before finding the courage to look at her again. "May I see the picture again?"

"Of course!" she replied. Traci reached for her purse and took the picture out of her wallet. She smiled and glanced at it a moment before passing it to me.

"He's beautiful," I said, smiling. "Can I keep this? Do you mind?"

"Absolutely."

I stared at the photo of my newly-discovered son. God, what a beautiful boy.

***

In the Minneapolis—St. Paul International Airport, Traci and I stood at the gate. I looked at the picture of Danny again.

"Well," I said, "I better get …"

"Yeah, me too," she cut in. "I want to grab a magazine or something before the next flight. I can meet you back here in a bit."

"Sure thing."

Traci reached in her purse for a pad and pencil and scribbled out a note. "Hey, before I forget or we lose sight of each other or something, here's Angelina's number. I'll talk to her when I see her and, well, let her know about you."

"Great. Thank you. I really mean it."

"It's my pleasure. Anything to make my sister happy."

"Well, I'm going to grab a bite to eat before this next flight. I'll be right back."

"Okay," she replied as she waved goodbye. I smiled as I walked away from her.

I lifted up the picture and took another look before walking over to the agent at the counter.

"Hi. May I help you?" the ticket agent asked.

"I'd like a ticket back to Portland," I replied, cramming the photo in my pocket.

TO Light a Fire 2

"The radical right is so homophobic that they're blaming global warming on the AIDS quilt."

Dennis Miller

It was a beautiful Monday at Your Name Here High School. The high school was arguably the worst school in the entire state of Oregon. The art teacher was known for coming to school high, there was no insulation in the hallways, and in the winter, it was so cold that the students could see their breath when walking from classes. The trig teacher would get halfway through a problem on the board, then couldn't figure out how to solve it and would say, "We'll come back to that," but never did. And in law class, the students watched videos about the mafia, Court TV, and other criminals and chases. Hell, there was even a special stairway dedicated to sex. The banner across the entrance of the school read: "Welcum Too Hii Skul."

The students took their seats in the James Bryant Gym for an assembly. James Bryant was the second principal of Your Name Here High School. He worked out every day, eating nothing but organic food. In fact, Bryant was one of the founding fathers of the organic food movement that swept the nation. He even enforced a rule at the school in which no junk food would be allowed on the premises.

One day, during an assembly, Bryant bragged that he would live until he was a hundred unless some sugar-crazed taxi driver killed him. Partway through the assembly, Bryant dropped dead due to a massive heart attack.

Mr. Bruce, the African-American science teacher, stood in the back with Ms. Streepova, arguably the smartest history teacher alive. With a short black bob and sexy reading glasses, she was the perfect, naughty teacher type.

"I love teaching," Streepova said to Bruce. "You realize that we may have the privilege of teaching the next Einstein, Newton, or Shakespeare?"

"Who cares?" Bruce replied. "I hope we teach the next American Idol. That would rock."

Streepova rolled her eyes. "Where's the principal?"

"He's on stage."

"That's not good. Remember the last time he had a microphone? He started doing a Chris Rock routine."

"I know. Although I thought it was funny that he replaced the word 'nigger' with 'nagger.' It was like watching an R-rated movie on network television."

The principal stood behind the microphone. "Good morning, Vietnam!" he cried out. None of the kids understood the reference. "Good Morning, Vietnam? Robin Williams? God, you guys suck. Well, anyways, we have a performance this afternoon by Jake Stanley, a member of Students Unite Against Alcohol. He's going to teach you the dangers of the truth syrup. Have fun."

The principal walked off the stage as Jake took the stage.

"Hey kids, are you ready for some real fun?!" Jake asked. The students did not respond. "Yeah! Sounds like it! You know what?" No response. "You kids rock! You guys are too cool for beer! Did you know that alcohol can damage every single organ in your body?!" No response. "Yeah, it does! Now I know you kids love raps. I would like to perform a rap for you all!"

The principal stood in the back with Streepova and Bruce.

The effects may be rad,
although alcohol is bad.

It may make you think that authority is cheesy,
but it will make you feel quite queasy.

If you go to school intoxicated,
your grades will drop and your housing will be debated.

You will sit in class, and time will pass,
but nothing will be taught and you'll be a dumb ass

Your pee will turn green,
to the bullies, you'll be mean.

Please do not drink,
it will change your perception and the way you think.

If an adult were to find you drunk,
on your head: a solid clunk.

Parties may be wild,
but they are not activities for a child.

So if you ever think of all the adventures you could have as you drink,
just think about the chairs, of which your bottoms will sink.

Finally, children, do you not see,
If you don't drink alcohol, you can be just like me!

The students all gaped in shock and horror. Bruce turned to the principal. "Where in the world did you get that virgin?"

"Bruce!" Streepova said.

"He is a virgin," the principal replied. "I completely agree with Bruce."

"I wonder how much he got paid?" Bruce asked.

"Probably minimum wage," the principal replied. "I would never, ever do that for a living."

"I'd rather be an electric chair tester in Texas," Bruce said.

"I'd rather be a lifeguard at a nude beach for seniors," the principal added.

Bruce and the principal looked at Streepova. "You got something?" Bruce asked her.

Streepova looked at both of them. "I'd rather be unemployed?"

The principal nodded. "Funny ... and topical. Very good."

Streepova smiled a little bit. Little did they know, she'd rather be unemployed than work at this school. This place was a dump.

***

After lunch, Streepova saw a bunch of students drinking beer in the hallway. She walked through the crowd and everyone had a can of beer in their hand. She spotted Kevin and Richard, two sophomores she knew well, and ran toward them.

"Hey, hey," Kevin said to Richard in a drunken slur, "did you know that most Americans can't identify Iraq on the map of the United States?"

"Idiots!" Richard replied as he struggled to remain upright. "Fucking idiots!"

Streepova grabbed the cans of beer from both students. "Boys! What's going on here?"

"I need my beer!" Kevin stumbled forward and tried to grab his beer. "It's good for the soul," Richard said with a goofy laugh. He pounded his chest for emphasis and almost knocked himself to the ground.

"Alcohol is bad for you," Streepova warned.

She ran into the principal's office and found the principal watching television. A can of Rusty's Beer was clutched firmly in his hand.

"Sir!" Streepova cried out.

"Hold on, Streepova, *Celebrity Fear Factor* is on. This week, the contestants are threatened with total anonymity."

Streepova turned off the TV. "What's going on here? The students are all drinking beer! And what are you doing drinking on school property?"

"Look, I needed a drink after watching that train-wreck of a performance. Man, I would have been way funnier than that."

"Sir, he was trying to explain to our students about the dangers of drinking."

"Well, look at them ... he did a great job, huh?"

"We have to do something!"

"Put them all in a cage," the principal said, taking another sip of his beer.

"We tried that last year. That didn't work so well now did it?"

"Yeah ... the school did blow up at the end of the day. Probably shouldn't try that again."

"You know that if we don't do something, the parents are going to come after us."

The principal choked on his beer and almost spit it out. "The parents?!"

"Yes, sir, the parents."

"Holy shit, they are the worst," he replied. "Remember when I drove some students over to the museum for that shitty field trip because the bus had broken down?"

"Yeah, you were texting on your cell phone while you were driving. You got busted for speeding."

"I had so many complaints that day! Damn parents."

"How fast were you going?"

"Like twenty-five or thirty words a minute."

"No, sir, speed of the car … you know… never mind. Look, I don't want to get complaints from the parents, so we need to do something to alleviate this. Plus, it's illegal!"

The principal emptied his beer can and reached over for another one. "You're right. And I've got the perfect idea."

Suddenly, the door burst open. A hoard of parents ran into the principal's office pushing Streepova out of the way. Ronald and Susan led the effort to take down the school.

"Your school made my daughter drunk!" Ronald complained.

"My son is drinking alcohol because of you!" Susan followed.

"Hold on, hold on," the principal said, trying to calm the hoard. "I understand your concern. This is a matter that is currently under review and we'll come up with an appropriate call to action in the upcoming days."

"Upcoming days?" Paul, another parent, complained.

"Yeah, what review?" Ronald asked. "My daughter's drinking beer. She's underage!"

"This is a serious issue that we are looking into very carefully," the principal said.

"Well, you better give us an answer now, or we're going to sue you for turning our children into alcoholics!"

The principal burped. "Listen, I'm upset about this situation as well. In fact, you know who I am upset at? Rusty's Beer. That's right, Rusty's Beer." He picked up the Rusty's beer can on his desk. "They shouldn't be promoting their beer to kids. Why, look at all of their beer cans in the hallway. It's a disgrace. Clearly, they don't care about your kids' well being."

"You're right!" Susan cried out. "Rusty's Beer is to blame!"

"Down with Rusty's!" Ronald yelled. "Let's kill him!"

The parents ran out of the principal's office. The principal smiled triumphantly at Streepova. "You can thank me later," he said as he picked up his can and guzzled down the rest of his beer.

***

The parents marched to the Rusty's Beer brewery. Rusty was watching the beer being made as the hoard of parents came in and surrounded him.

"What's going on?" Rusty asked.

"You made our kids drunk!" Ronald cried out.

"My son had to be taken to the hospital today because of you!" Susan yelled.

"What? Us?" Rusty asked.

"Well … yeah … you," Ronald said.

"Hold on a second. We don't sell our beer here. The Quickie-Mart sells our beer."

Ronald thought about it for a second. "That's a good point. Somehow, the beer has to make it to the kids' hands."

"That store is selling beer to minors! What bastards!" Susan yelled.

"Let's kill them!" Ronald cried out.

The parents all marched from Rusty's Beer. Rusty looked confounded by the whole scene. "They'll be back," he said to himself.

***

The parents marched over to the Quickie-Mart where the manager Jon was cleaning the counter. Jon was stunned by the number of people who filed into his tiny store.

"What's going on?" he asked.

"You sold beer to our kids!" Ronald cried out.

"Yeah, my son's in the hospital because of you!" Susan yelled.

"Hold on a second," Jon said, "don't blame Quickie-Mart."

"And why the hell not?" Susan asked.

"We don't sell beer to minors," he replied. "This state has a very strict policy against that. Why would I want to lose my store for six bucks?"

"Good point," Ronald replied.

"We only sell our beer to people over twenty-one … adults," Jon said.

"Damn adults. Let's blame them!" Ronald yelled.

"They sent my son to the hospital!" Susan yelled louder.

"Wait a minute," said Paul, another parent. "We are the adults."

"Oh shit, you're right," Ronald said.

"I didn't send my son to the hospital!" Susan yelled.

"Yeah, we're good parents. We couldn't have done it," Ronald said.

"We have to do something," Paul said. "We could be in deep trouble."

Ronald thought about it. "Well, we didn't drink the beer. Our kids did! Let's blame our kids!"

"Yeah! My son took my ... son ... wait ... he sent himself to the hospital because of himself. Yeah!" Susan cried out.

"Let's kill ... err ... punish them!" Ronald yelled.

***

The parents marched back to the school and entered the gym where several kids were playing sports.

"Hey kids!" Ronald yelled.

"What's going on?" Jeremy, a freshman, asked.

"All of you caused my kid to drink beer," Susan said.

"My daughter is going to have to go to AA because of you guys!" Ronald protested.

"Don't blame me for your daughter's alcohol problem," Jeremy replied.

Another freshman, Julia, walked over to Jeremy. "What's going on?" she asked.

"These parents are blaming us for getting their kids drunk," Jeremy said.

"Don't blame us," Julia replied.

"Did you drink the beer?" Ronald asked.

"I did," Julia said.

"Me, too," Jeremy added.

"Well, why did you do it?" Susan asked.

"I guess you guys didn't see the assembly earlier today," Jeremy said. "There was this awful virgin who rapped that if we stopped drinking beer, we could be like him."

"The thing is, we don't want to be like him," Julia said. "He's the biggest douchebag since Ryan Seacrest."

"Damn ... that's a douchebag," Ronald said. "Well, let's blame him!"

"Let's kill him!" Susan cried out.

The parents all ran out of the gym. Jeremy and Julia shook their heads in pure embarrassment.

"I hope we don't end up acting like them," Jeremy said.

***

Inside Whole Foods, the parents walked up to Jake who was putting some groceries in his shopping cart.

"We caught you!" Ronald cried out.

"Prepare to die!" Susan yelled.

"What's going on?" Jake asked.

"We know what you did," Ronald said. "Your extremely pathetic lyrics caused our children to drink alcohol."

"I'm a member of Students Unite Against Alcohol," he replied. "We prevent children from drinking that horrible liquid."

"Well, you did a lousy job," Paul said.

"My son is in the hospital because of you," Susan said.

"Don't blame me for your son being in the hospital," Jake said.

Susan was about to punch him, but Paul and Ronald held her back. "I'm going to kill you!" she cried out. "Rip you to pieces!"

"Ma'am, I told him not to drink," Jake said. "Look, blame the school. They hired me to perform at their gym."

Susan stopped. "You're right. The school did hire you to rap those pathetic lyrics."

"I don't really think my lyrics were pathetic."

"You're right," Ronald said. "The school paid money for this douchebag with no life to rap."

"I wouldn't consider myself a douchebag …"

"Let's go to the school!" Paul exclaimed.

"Let's kill them!" Susan cried out.

The parents stormed out of the Whole Foods grocery store. Jake shook his head as he pushed his shopping cart to the checkout.

***

The parents stormed into the principal's office with pitchforks in hands. Streepova was seated before the principal's desk.

"What's going on?" the principal asked.

"We blame the school!" Ronald cried out.

"Yeah! The school made our kids drunk!" Susan cried out more.

"Whoa, whoa, slow down old people," the principal replied. "It's not our fault."

"Then whose fault is it?" Ronald asked.

The principal looked at Streepova. She shrugged. She could tell that the principal was thinking of a way out of this mess.

"Blame Rusty's Beer!" the principal replied.

"Rusty's Beer?" Ronald asked.

"Yes, Rusty's Beer. The kids are drinking it. Why not blame them?"

Ronald thought about it for a second. "Yeah … you're right! Come on, guys, let's blame Rusty's Beer!"

"Down with Rusty's!" Susan cried out.

"Let's kill him!" Ronald exclaimed.

The students at Your Name Here High School watched from the windows, in a drunken haze, as their parents stormed off, pitchforks in hand.

opportunity of a Lifetime

"Media is a word that has come to mean bad journalism."

Graham Greene

It was a surprising sunny day in the City of Roses. People were flocking to Tom McCall Waterfront Park to stay cool in its refreshing water fountain. Without forewarning, it got darker. No, it wasn't gray clouds coming in.

The people looked up into the sky and saw a large spaceship. It was long and narrow, and several beams of light shot out from above.

People screamed in horror as they ran away from its shadow. A hoard of reporters from all four major news stations scurried to the scene. They set up their cameras around the shadow and the reporters tested out their microphones to make sure they were working properly.

Suddenly, a beam of light shined on the fountain. The spaceship hovered for a minute and then a door creaked open. The crowd hushed at what was unfolding before their eyes.

An alien was emerging from the spaceship. It had three round eyes, canine claws on its four arms, and butterfly-shaped wings sprung from its back. The alien landed on the ground and started crawling around quickly, like a trapped mouse. With its three eyes, it observed all of the cameras flashing in its direction.

The alien stood up and started making several strange beeping sounds. The reporters looked at each other and at their crews in confusion.

The alien raised one of its arms and created a peace sign with its clawed fingers.

"I come in peace," it said.

Everyone turned to their neighbor and spoke in hushed tones. No one knew what to say to the extraterrestrial.

One of the reporters, Judith Tuck, finally broke from the pack and walked up to the creature. "Welcome to our planet."

The alien looked at her. "Lovely city you have here."

"What are you doing here?" she asked.

"I am here to help you humans."

Cameras started to flash even more than ever. Judith wrote the information down on a notepad. "Help us with what?" she asked.

"I want to give you the cure for cancer," it replied, blinking each of its eyes individually and repeatedly.

"The cure for cancer?" Judith repeated.

"Yes. Now, if you all could give me a minute of your time, I will let you know the formula."

All of the reporters took out their notepads and gave the alien their undivided attention.

Suddenly, Judith's cell phone rang, startling everyone including the alien.

The alien pulled out a weapon that looked like a laser gun from its utility belt. "What is that?"

The crowd yelled in horror and ducked for cover.

Judith kept her eyes on the alien and moved extremely slowly as she removed the cell phone from her pocket. "Just a cell phone … a cell phone …" she nervously replied.

The alien placed the gun back in it's holster. "I thought it was a weapon. My apologies. I come in peace."

Judith answered her ringing phone. "Hello? … yes, I'm here. What's going on? Are you serious?! Really?! Oh, my God, I'll be right there." She hung up.

"What was that?" the alien asked.

"I have to go," she replied.

The alien furrowed its face and looked confused. "You have to go? Go where?"

Suddenly, the cell phones of all the other reporters rang. They all answered their cells.

"What is going on?" the alien asked again, as Judith started packing her gear.

The other reporters hung up and quickly packed up their equipment. The cameramen packed up their cameras as fast as they could and ran back to their respective news vans.

"Wait! Where are you all going?" the alien asked.

Judith wiped the sweat off her forehead and looked at the creature. "Brad Pitt is at Pioneer Courthouse Square with a new woman!" she replied, smiling.

The alien looked confused. "Who's Brad Pitt?"

The reporters quickly ran away from the scene.

"Who's Brad Pitt?" the alien asked again. "Is he your leader?"

A minute later, nobody was within fifty yards of the alien. They were all racing to Brad Pitt's alleged whereabouts.

The alien shook its head in disbelief. "Fucking douchebags," it shouted as a beam of light shined on its body. The alien floated up the beam and back into the spaceship.

Sold/Bought/Mine

"A painting in a museum hears more ridiculous opinions than anything else in the world."

Edmond de Goncourt

"I honestly couldn't tell you what happened," said a wide-eyed Sean Hunter. "This is the first time a piece has been stolen from the museum."

Three burly men and a petite woman with her hair tied back in a tight bun were scattered around a rectangular table in the basement security center of the Portland Art Museum. The cops created levels, each standing at a slightly different angle, posed with their arms in different ways. They all wore the same uniforms, sported the same badges and equipment, and all had the same, unenthused facial expression.

It was 3:45 AM and a modest segment of the city police force had just arrived at the museum to investigate a reported theft. No one could justify what was going on. The museum had been locked as usual, the security system solidly in place. The art pieces were all successfully armed in case of removal, and no alarm had gone off at all. It was understandable how shocked and appalled everyone was to find out that a night guard had inexplicably discovered an empty 2-foot by 3-foot space on the wall of the most recently-installed temporary modern art gallery. Without a trace, the newest Miranda Petere had simply vanished.

"Sean, explain it to me one more time. It's just ... gone?" Dr. Drummond, President of the museum's Board of Directors, leered at Sean quizzically and condescendingly through his low-set glasses. His bald spot glistened in the film-noir lighting of the cavernous basement room. I was standing on the balcony, behind a column, hidden from view.

Sean still did not look up from the titanium table. He spoke mechanically with a subtle hint of desperation, or perhaps the desperation was a trick of his unblinking gaping eyes. The truth was, the static level of his voice was quite convincingly calm.

"I told you, Harold," Sean said, "the guard was making his rounds as usual. He came across the empty space. He didn't report anything suspicious, he didn't hear anything, see anyone out of the ordinary. There was no malfunction with the security system. It must have been removed sometime between 1:00 and 1:30, but we have no idea how. As soon as he noticed the painting was gone, he and the team called me. They did a complete sweep of the building. When I got here, we did another. There is no trace of the painting anywhere, and I have no idea what happened."

Beads of sweat were forming just below Sean's hairline. I could also tell that he was shaking, just a little.

I was taken aback by the theft, but no one was feeling it more than Sean. The Moderns Gallery had been his idea from the get-go, and he wasn't like most board members. Sean knew his stuff. Even more than that, he cared. He had some insight. Several people on the PAM Board of Directors were stuffy businessmen and women who only really had financial and commodity issues on their minds when designing their exhibitions. It really made me sick that people like *that* got to choose what was art nowadays. Honestly, the first time I met the creative team for the Moderns display, I thought I had walked into the wrong bar!

We were meeting for drinks to discuss what would be going into the exhibit, and I couldn't find the booth because I was apparently looking for the wrong, shall we say, *type* of personnel. It came as no surprise that the people I'd imagined as the casting directors for an exhibit of this caliber would be slightly different from the crowd you'd normally find walking about downtown Portland at 9PM on a Thursday evening. Maybe there'd be a pair of horn-rimmed glasses in the mix, perhaps a handmade vest or skirt, or maybe, I don't know, a splash of color somewhere in the bunch. I was hoping something would set them apart from the regular, everyday bar patrons. They were all in business suits. Quite literally, they were a bunch of suits, deciding the fate of the first modern art exhibit in the PAM. I was mortified. But then I noticed Sean.

Off in the corner of the booth, looking slightly out of place and uncomfortable, Sean sat gazing dreamily at the coaster underneath his wine glass. When I asked him about it later, he went off on a tangent about how the glass distorted the colors and produced such an interesting visual effect. He was drinking not a Gin and Tonic or Scotch on the rocks like his colleagues, but red wine in a large glass that must have been the size of my head. Yes, when I saw Sean, I knew that he was just a little bit different from the others, but I didn't know until later just how massive that rift was.

Sean Hunter completed his undergraduate degree at the MFA in Boston. He got his MBA at Indiana, then a PhD in Art History from

Stanford just a few years later. He was young, sharp, and devilishly handsome, not to mention passionate and knowledgeable. Also, he wouldn't want me saying this, but he dabbled in neo-cubist painting, and could probably pass his work off as an original Braque or early Duchamp, at least to undergraduate art students. Sean had all the talent in the world, he just worried about his own innovation. In short, Sean Hunter was who I thought deserved to be working on this project. I guess I was biased, though, because I was also a little bit in love with him from the moment I saw him in that corner of the booth. My type, I guess.

But yes, Sean was horrified by the fact that the Petere was stolen because he had spent quite a long time trying to procure that piece. It was called "Sold," and played a lot with light and color in a way that a lot of people were critical of. The artist had been inspired by the light falling on a huge mansion near where she lived. Unfortunately, in this economy, it wasn't selling despite its grandeur, prime location, and utter beauty. It was one of her favorites. There wasn't a ton of hype about the piece. Petere was a new artist, just breaking onto the scene, but Sean liked the piece, and wanted it in the exhibit, probably more as a symbol than anything else — the change and rebirth associated with modern art. It was, after all, the first contemporary exhibit in the PAM. The artist had been stubborn about putting it in after meeting the aforementioned board, but no one could say no to Sean forever; his charm and know-how were completely impossible to circumvent.

After the report was filed and the police left, it was nearly 6AM and the museum would be opening in just a few hours. I had walked up the stairs to the atrium where the PAM was putting on their modest little Moderns exhibit. Gentle gold and red hues were drifting through the glass panels above me, coloring the floor below. The room looked like a Rothko. For just a second, I felt a little guilty, walking on a Rothko. It seemed disrespectful somehow.

Footsteps echoed through the gallery, ricocheting off the frames and glass cases. I turned to see Sean ascending the staircase behind me, looking worn and defeated.

"Seany," I said, puffing out my lower lip and offering him what I imagined looked like a deep pair of puppy dog eyes. You never really knew what your facial expressions looked like to other people, but I was fairly certain that face had worked on him before. "Sean, don't you worry, it's not your fault."

"I know Miranda," he said, "it's just such a shame about the painting. It added so much to the gallery." He draped his arm around my shoulder, and it came along with more weight than I thought it would.

"I think we both know it didn't quite fit anyway," I said jovially, but not infectiously so. "And I'll tell you one thing," I continued, leaning into his shoulder and cupping one hand around his ear, "the artist isn't mad."

He laughed, and I smiled. "Thanks, I'm glad there're no hard feelings," he replied. "I know you loved that one."

He dragged me around in a circle so we could descend the staircase. I glanced behind me. The color flooding the room from the sunrise was gentler now. Probably more like what Rothko would have decided on, although I couldn't know for sure.

"The police are going to do the best they can to find it. We'll get it back," he said.

"Maybe," I said dreamily, still gazing at the ocean of pastel morning colors in our wake.

Sean walked me out the door and to my car. He said he needed to fill out some more insurance paperwork, but I should get home safely and come by the gallery in the afternoon for an update. I nodded amiably, but knew there wouldn't be time because of a lunch with an agent for a gallery uptown. He kissed me goodbye and trudged back to the museum.

Once Sean was safely inside, I opened the tinted driver's seat door of my Mini Cooper and half-smiled at the painting resting in the passenger seat. It looked okay in the PAM, but I knew it was going to look so much better in my bedroom.

Peaked Early

"They say that time changes things, but you actually have to change them yourself."

Andy Warhol

James Cosgrove walked into an unlit Hillsboro bar and looked around nervously, experiencing all too vividly a retreat to his former grade school self — feeling alone and friendless, without a place to put down his lunch tray in the cafeteria. His eyes bounced from figure to figure as he tried to make out facial features of the people surrounding him. It wasn't easy to focus on a single trajectory since he wasn't exactly sure what to be looking for. It had been nearly a decade since he had seen most of his classmates from Hillsboro High School, and while he could distinctly remember what most of his once-close friends looked like, James had no way of knowing what they looked like now.

Finally, a flash of scarlet red, royal blue, and white caught James' eye. Hillsboro High colors: the proud mark of the Hillsboro Spartans. James smiled at the thought of his former mascot running around at football games and drinking beer out of Coke bottles and vodka out of hip flasks with his friends underneath the stands. He approached the modest group of people huddled in a booth over a few pitchers of beer. Suddenly, the dark, oppressive curtain over the bar was lifted, and the low hum of banter and chatter was completely overwhelmed by a sudden roar of yells and cries.

"James, man! So good to see you!" said one former student.

"Jim, it's been so long. Too long!" another said.

"James, you look great. The years have been good to you!" a third commented.

He was overwhelmed by the generic sentences flowing out of his friends' mouths, like rivers of words that had been dammed up for too long and finally released. He buckled under the weight of his slightly-intoxicated peers showering him with embraces, handshakes, and gentle, playful punches in the shoulder and abdomen. His personal space was briefly nonexistent, and his body wasn't used to getting pummeled like it was in high school. However, James could not shed the impossibly wide grin plastered over his face.

With a big sigh of comfort and pleasure, James collapsed into a chair at the end of the table, and began to soak in the sight of his friends clustered in the booth, all gazing at him with his same bright, relieved, undyingly happy expression. It was good to be home.

As the night went on and the drinks flowed freely, James listened intently and chimed in when appropriate as his friends recounted their exploits since school. Mark was married with three children, working as an investment banker at a big firm in Washington. No surprise there, he was excellent at math in high school and president of the finance club. James giggled to himself as they all reminisced about young Mark, investing in stock at the age of 16. He went through a brief stint where he wore business suits to school on days when the investment club met.

Margaret ended up marrying her high school sweetheart, David. They both sat to James's left, her hand gently resting near his elbow, probably unconsciously. Margaret and David had been together on and off for years before finally deciding to tie the knot. But they had been in each other's lives for so long, there was magnetism between them — a subtle, automatic dance they did, interacting without meaning to. It was beautiful to behold.

Henry had moved away to Chicago. He was a teacher now in the French school there. Henry had gone through a rough patch near the end of high school — almost didn't graduate — but he'd pulled himself together in the years afterwards. He smiled modestly as he demonstrated each of the four languages he could speak fluently.

Hanging on to his friends' words, James glowed with interest and pride at each account of their accomplishments. He laughed at their comical stories about kids, pets, and employers.

Finally, Henry turned to James. "Jim, what have you been up to? You were the smartest out of all of us. First in the class, right? You dork," Henry said affectionately, jabbing James in the abdomen with his elbow and inciting a quick wave of laughter from the table.

Without missing a beat except to massage his slightly bruised rib, James replied, "Oh you know. Same old."

"Oh come on, Jim," Henry persisted. "Anyone special? Work going well? What's going on with you, dude?"

James took another drink and swallowed. "Oh you know, still live around here. Haven't met the right girl yet, I guess. Work's okay."

His ambiguity was disappointing, but James had never been very outspoken. As he shrugged off the interrogation, Matthew jumped in. "Bachelor, eh? Don't sweat it, me too. Can't tie this one down!" he shouted, louder than one should in a bar, but his distasteful behavior was overlooked by the buzzed patrons.

The small group of alumni laughed enthusiastically, taking his shift in the conversation and running with it. It appeared James was off the hook.

***

The last call bell rang for the second time, and the manager turned on the lights. James's friends groaned emphatically, dragging themselves up from the mahogany table. They all stumbled out to the curb, nursing their last drinks that would probably go unfinished.

"Well," said David, supporting a very drunk Margaret with his left arm and shoulder, "we'd best get back to the hotel. Got an early flight back to San Fran tomorrow and work on Monday. It's been great to catch up. We should do this again soon!"

Through yawns, the friends said their goodbyes, exchanging kisses, hugs, handshakes, and promises to keep in better touch. One by one, everyone hailed cabs or stumbled to the bus stop around the corner.

Henry, being as enthusiastic as he was about catching up, was the last left standing with James on the corner. "You gonna get home okay, buddy? Need me to call you a cab?" Henry was considerably more intoxicated than James, placing perhaps more of his body weight than he intended behind the hand resting on James's chest.

"I'm good to walk, thanks," James replied. "It's been great seeing you."

"Don't be a stranger, Jim! I know where you live!" That was a lie, but lies didn't quite count if they couldn't be recalled in the morning.

Once Henry was comfortably in a cab en route to his bed and breakfast, James put both hands in his pockets, and began trudging down the street toward the park. He squinted looking up at the bleak, overcast night sky, and felt a rain drop on his forehead just above his left eyebrow. It was followed by a few more until the sounds of a light shower and passing cars were all that filled James' ears. He shuddered and walked faster, finally reaching the park's outer gates.

Once inside, he traced the serpentine trail leading toward the center, and finally found his familiar bench and the two elm trees that framed it. He bent down and reached into a deep hole at the base of the right hand tree, and removed a windbreaker and a tattered old golf umbrella.

133

Once James was zipped up and hooded safely under the umbrella, he reached into the burrow again and drew out a wool blanket, which he delicately lay out over the park bench. He lay down on top of it, stabilizing the umbrella in the planks of the bench so it wouldn't fall over or blow away. James briefly considered making his way over to the shelter for the evening, since the rain appeared to be picking up, but there was no sign of thunder or lightning, so he let his mind ease into equilibrium. The damp breeze flowed over his legs, rustling the shrubbery around him, and blowing the October leaves from his two elms.

As James closed his eyes, he saw the Hillsboro Spartans all lined up on the football field, Margaret and Dave cheering them on beside him in the stands, Henry and Mark on the other side. Behind a flood of red, blue, and white, James fell asleep to the sounds of trumpets ringing in an astounding victory at the homecoming game.

Blink Death Away

"You have a choice. Live or die. Every breath is a choice. Every minute is a choice. To be or not to be."

Chuck Palahniuk

The floor is cold. It feels like linoleum, but it could be the hardwood floor in my dining room. I would know if I could reach up or down, but I seem to have lost control of all of my limbs. The last thing that's burned into my memory is a man … my friend, Lucas. He stopped by for a drink. Maybe … A drink …

The familiar screeching sound of a key scratching against the inside of the door reaches my ear, accompanied soon after by a voice. "Anna! Honey, I'm home, did you walk the dog?"

What's going on? I yearn to answer him, but no matter how hard I try, my lips don't move. My husband, Jackson, the owner of the voice, begins to walk. His loafers produce a clearly identifiable squeak against the linoleum in the kitchen.

Linoleum in the kitchen. I must be in the dining room, but why am I on the floor?

"Anna? Anna where are you?" he continues through the house until … "Oh my God! Anna! Anna, can you hear me?"

Yes, of course I can hear you, but why the hell can't I answer you? Still no sound. I hear Jackson rush to the floor next to me. I can feel his warm hands on my face. He lifts up my eyelids which were closed until now. I can see him. The utter fear in his face, the sheer terror at the thought of losing me.

Losing me.

Could I … Could I be dead? No, of course not, how could I be dead? Dead people can't see or hear. *Could they?* No, never, dead is dead, my organs couldn't function if I was dead and I think I'm alive. Dead people can't think. Dead people can't breathe. Dead people can't … *Am I not breathing?* The thought hadn't occurred to me yet. I can feel myself doing it, I think.

"Anna! Don't you leave me!" I feel him begin compressions on my chest. I see him look down at my chest and then check my pulse. His eyes were watering.

Jackson dear, CPR DOESN'T WORK on people who are STILL ALIVE! WHY CAN'T YOU SEE THAT I'M ALIVE?

He stopped. Why did he stop? Why is he crying? He pulls himself to his feet and walks away. *Where's he going now?* I hear his loafers padding across the dining room, living room, and kitchen. He reaches for the phone and I can hear him take it off the hook to dial.

"Hello? Portland Police? My … my wife, something happened to my wife, she's not breathing and I can't find a pulse. Dead? I don't KNOW!! Why don't you come down here and give me some help, that's what you get PAID for right? I'm sorry I'm … thank you … Jackson Powell. Her name's Anna. Anna Powell. Yes, and please hurry. I don't know how much time she has. Thank you."

He runs back through the house to my side and checks my pulse again.

What happened?

He only came for a drink. I've known Lucas for years, why would he do that?

Dead people can't feel. Dead people can't think. I'm not dead, I can't be dead.

But how did he do it? How did Lucas …

Kill me.

I hear a siren come down the street. *Wow that was fast.* Jackson runs to open the door. What sounds like a considerably large herd of EMTs and police officers file rapidly into the living room.

"Can you tell us where the body is Mr. Powell?" one of the EMTs asks.

"Please don't call her that, and she's in the dining room," Jackson replies.

The EMT calls his colleagues and they run to where I'm lying motionless on the floor. Someone thinks to turn on the chandelier and light floods into my unblinking eyes. It burns a little. I think my pupils contract, but no one notices. I see a stranger, a man I think, crouch down next to me. The smell of latex and rubbing alcohol fills my nostrils. The man shines a bright flashlight into my eyes.

"Pupils are fully dilated," the EMT said. Oh well. At least that explains the burning. He puts two fingers on my neck to feel my pulse. "No cause of death apparent …"

CAUSE OF DEATH????

"Some bruises on the abdominal region," he continued. "It looks like she might have hit her head on the table too and suffered a slight concussion before …"

I remember. Lucas was talking about high school … the prom. We were going as friends but he … he wanted to finish what he started. I screamed. He pushed me, and I fell onto the dining room table. *But that wouldn't have killed me, not that I'm dead ...*

The drinks.

As the EMTs fussed over me, I hear Jackson talking to a CSI agent, "I don't know what could have happened, she was supposed to be home all day. She had a little cold. I guess she fell or something, but I don't know. Is she going to be okay?"

I'll be fine Jackson, relax.

"I mean I don't know what I'll do, she's my life. We don't even have life insurance."

"Mr. Powell," the CSI agent said, "I'm afraid your wife is no longer with us."

DEAD?! I'M NOT DEAD! WHY CAN'T YOU SEE THAT I'M ALIVE!!

"No, there's no way, you must have made a mistake," Jackson said.

"I'm so sorry Mr. Powell. I know what you must be going through, but you can begin the healing process sooner if we can figure out why this happened and you can accept the fact that Anna has passed on. She would have wanted you to ..."

"How do you know what she would have wanted?" he yells. "Now, you re-examine her because my wife is not dead!"

Good, Jackson.

The EMTs disregard Jackson's pleas and recruit a few members to go out to the ambulance.

What the hell did Lucas put in those drinks?

It sounds like the EMTs are coming back now. I feel two of them lift up my body, which feels heavy and solid, not unlike a slab of lumber. They drop me back down, not exactly gently, on something that feels like rubber. It smells like something else though. I hear a zipper being drawn up close to my feet.

Are they putting me in a body bag?

Jackson obviously realizes what is going on and runs to stop the EMTs from zipping me up.

Anna, it's now or never, I think, *now you know you're not dead, but they don't know you're not dead, and Jackson isn't going to be able to fight them forever. You have to do something.* I search for a way to create a sign

— make sound, a motion, anything to convince them of my current state. I muster up all of my energy, more than I ever knew I had, and channel it to my mouth. *Wwwww ... wwwwww. God, Helen Keller was a brilliant woman. Wwww ...*

"Wwwwww."

A rush of air comes through my mouth. I whistle, using every bit of strength I have.

"WAIT, STOP!" Jackson yells. "Did you see that? Did you hear that?"

"What?"

"She whistled, Anna whistled, she's alive!"

"Mr. Powell, I know it's hard, but she's really not. Dead people don't whistle."

No kidding. Suddenly I regain the use of my face. *Ha. Lucas' poison, or whatever, must be wearing off.* I blink. I blink again.

"Mr. Powell, I'm going to have to ask you to step away from your wife." He turns to me. "Holy Mary Mother of God! She's blinking!"

Dead people don't blink.

Losing Mrs. Right

"Sex relieves tension – love causes it."

Woody Allen

Daryl Whitten stared outside the window of his downtown Portland apartment. *So many beautiful women out there*, he thought as he watched the crowds of people going about their way. The 26-year-old high school biology teacher longed to run out and introduce himself to half of them.

But he knew most of them were probably married or in a serious relationship. Daryl had never minded cheating if the sex was good, but he always seem to meet the girls who believed in fidelity, being honest, and staying committed.

"All the women in Portland and I can't find one to settle down with," he moaned.

Stanley Ross popped the top off the third beer. It was only two o'clock, but it was a Saturday and it was a long time until work on Monday morning. The two had been roommates since Stanley's divorce more than two years ago and they generally got along thanks in part to their belief in the three things that mattered most to a man — sex, alcohol, and sports. In their world, a perfect afternoon began with a woman serving them beer and pretzels, followed by sex in front of the television, and then the woman remaining silent during the rest of the game.

"You know what your problem is?" Stanley asked Daryl.

Daryl ignored his roommate.

Stanley asserted the question again. "Do you know what your problem is?"

"My roommate has a penis instead of a vagina?"

"Nah man, you're over-analyzing things," Stanley said. "Your problem is that you want to settle down and still play the field. You want a relationship that's like a Chinese buffet."

"Huh?"

"You want a relationship. That's the restaurant, the physical building," Stanley continued. "But you want to have sex with as many different women as possible, in as many ways as possible. So that's like the buffet. You can get as much as you want, of as many different items as possible."

Daryl shook his head in confusion.

"So you take the sweet and sour chicken," Stanley continued. "That's like the redhead you slept with last week. Then you got your egg rolls.

143

That's similar to the tiny Hawaiian girl one of your teacher friends set you up with. So you know, you're just sampling all of the foods in one restaurant and you're never hard up. That's why you've got to look at your love life like a buffet. Who needs a relationship? You're playing the field and the field is your restaurant."

"Yeah, right," Daryl said. "There's only one problem."

"What's that?"

"A lot of times my failure to stay with anyone longer than a night means I end up playing with myself the next night."

"Well, think of that as eating-in for a change."

Daryl sighed and shook his head. Oh, the times he had left the girls. There had been many times he had broken their hearts. The women wanted him, but he was still young and needed to play the field. Besides, he was a man. Men were made to play around. Even if it resulted in being lonely.

"Whatever happened to Mrs. Robinson, anyway?" Stanley asked.

Daryl had been sleeping with a woman old enough to be his mother, if not older, that he had met at a charity auction two months ago. She was fit for her age, the sex was good, and Daryl gave little thought to the reality that he was still spitting out crushed peas the first time she went down on a guy. Her name was Mrs. Benson, but Stanley liked to tease his buddy by likening her to the character in *The Graduate*.

"Oh, I don't know," Daryl said. "You know."

"You don't know what?"

"We only call each other when one of us is desperate. I like sex with women and she likes the idea of having sex with a young virile guy like me, rather than the old, fat men her age that can't get it up."

"That's easy to understand."

"What'd you mean?"

"I've got to think that I would enjoy a night with a young, lean guy like you who could keep it up all night," Stanley said.

"You would?"

"I mean, if I was a woman. If I was a woman!"

The two were silent for awhile. Daryl pondered his situation. Tonight was going to be the night that he found her. Commitment scared the hell out of him, but so did spending the rest of his life wandering from pasture to pasture. Fidelity sucked, but so did not having a female around on a regular basis.

"I think I'm gonna head over to the Pearl District later tonight," Daryl said. "You wanna come?"

"Nah, I think I'll just veg out here for the rest of the day. I've got plenty of beer, frozen Chinese food in the refrigerator, and there's a marathon of *America's Funniest Home Videos* on television."

***

Daryl knew she was the one the minute he saw her. She must be new to town because he had frequented every bar in the Pearl District a hundred times, but he had never seen her. But there she was: tall, blonde, and incredibly sensual. His gaze didn't go unnoticed by her or the three other girls that were with her.

It wasn't long before Daryl approached the quartet and began talking, but his eyes were only focused on the blonde who leaned in after a few minutes of small talk.

"I have my own car if you want to go somewhere else," she whispered.

"Sure, how about we get out of here and have a drink somewhere else? Maybe next door?"

"Why not?"

"What's your name?"

"Marian. And yours?"

"Daryl."

It only took a few seconds for Marian to say goodbye to her friends before the two made a hasty retreat from the bar to a smaller, quieter club a few doors down where they could have more privacy and talk.

"So, you do this often?" Daryl asked as they sat down at the bar.

"Do what often?"

"Leave the company of your friends to hook up with a guy you've just met?"

"Sometimes," Marian said. "Probably not as often as you though."

"Huh?"

"I've seen you before, Daryl. I didn't know your name, but me and my girlfriends see you out a lot and you're always leaving with the flavor of the night."

145

"You have? Why have I never seen you before?"

"You have, I just wasn't wearing a blonde wig."

"A wig? You're wearing a wig? Wow, you look good in it."

"I look good out of it, too."

"Yeah, I'm sure you do."

"We've seen you many nights before with different women, always hoping that we'd be the prize you'd take home," Marian said. "Who would have thought that a blonde wig was all it took to make you horny? You ever think about settling down with a woman?"

"Sure, all the time," Daryl said. "It's just that I like being wild and it's hard to settle on just one model. I mean, one woman."

Marian laughed. "Listen, cowboy, settling down doesn't mean you can't have lots of fun. Why do you think there are so many books and manuals out there to bring variety to couples' sex lives? And if the toys we bring into our playpen aren't enough, I can always wear a different wig every night."

Daryl blushed, both embarrassed and attracted to her aggressiveness.

"Yeah, I guess that would be fun," Daryl said.

"It would make an honest man out of you, too. A kinky man, but one that's honorable. What would your mommy and daddy say if they knew what a wild buck you were?"

"Mom? Mom would be horrified," Daryl said. "Dad, on the other hand, would have to admit that he was proud I had grown up in his footsteps."

"Dad gets around, huh?"

"Oh yeah."

"And your parents are still married?"

"Thirty-one years, faithfully!"

"Which is why you need to settle down, just like dear old dad," Marian said.

Daryl thought about his parents. Both him and his mother knew that his dad fooled around here and there, and Daryl often wondered why his mother stayed. Was it because of the stability? The embarrassment? They appeared to be happy, but maybe that was just it, an appearance. Who knew if his mother lay in bed crying herself to sleep while Dad was out fucking other women.

"Want to take me out for a test drive?" Marian snapped Daryl out of his thoughts.

"What? I mean, yeah. Sure."

"You said back at the other bar that you're a biology teacher. You ever teach your kids anatomy?"

"Uh-huh. We touch on anatomy every now and then."

"You want to touch on my anatomy?"

Daryl almost spit out the beer he had just swallowed. *Whoa Nellie*, he thought. *I'm supposed to be the instigator here.*

Marian laughed at the embarrassed look on his face. "Aww, you're blushing again. How cute!"

The sound of his cell phone ringing brought relief to Daryl's predicament. His relief faded when he looked at the caller ID: Doris Benson. Daryl hurriedly put away the phone without taking the call.

"Who is it?" Marian asked.

"Uh, no one," Daryl said, stammering. "Just some old broad that likes to use me as a boy toy every now and then."

Marian laughed. "Wow, you really do play the field, don't you?"

"You know, it beats staying at home alone."

"And day old bread is better than no bread, right?"

"In this case, moldy bread is better than no bread."

"I got a better idea," Marian said. "Why don't we head back to my place and I'll let you sample some fresh baked bread there?"

***

"I'm going to my bedroom," Marian said after they walked inside her house.

"Yeah, and I'm going with you," Daryl replied.

"No, I mean give me a few minutes first." Marian brushed him away. "Don't worry, lover, I wouldn't have brought you this far to dump you now."

Daryl watched as she disappeared down the hall. "Okay, but don't take long," he shouted.

The response almost immediately afterward caught him by surprise. It wasn't Marian's voice and it sounded as if it was coming from the kitchen instead of the direction in which she had disappeared.

"Daryl?"

"Yeah?" Daryl replied.

An older woman stepped into the living room. "Well, this is a surprise," Doris said. "When you didn't take my call, I thought I'd be stuck with someone older tonight. And how in the world did you find me here?"

Daryl was speechless. He had ignored her call at the bar, but how did she find him? "What are you doing here?"

"I'm staying here tonight. What are you doing here?"

Marian's voice came from down the hallway. "Who are you talking to, Daryl?"

"Hold on, I'm coming right now!" Daryl exclaimed.

"You're what?" Marian yelled.

"I mean I, I mean I …" Daryl dropped his voice to a whisper. He looked at Doris. "What do you mean you're staying here tonight? Does Marian know that?"

"I guess she'll find out in a few minutes. That's why I called you. The electricity went out at my house and I needed a place to stay. You blew me off and she wouldn't take a phone call from me, so I came over here."

"You called Marian tonight? What time?"

"Right after I called you. Why, is that a problem?"

"She? You? You're her…?"

"Her mother. Why, is that a problem?"

"Oh, Lord."

"What are you doing here, anyway? How do you know Marian?"

Daryl paused. "I'm here to touch Marian's anatomy."

"What?"

"I mean, teach Marian anatomy, that's all. You know I'm a biology teacher!"

Marian exited from her bedroom in a slinky pink lingerie slip and stopped. "Mother, what are you doing here?"

"What is he doing here, Marian?" Doris asked.

"He's here to …" Marian hesitated in her reply. "Wait, how do you know him?"

"We met two months, I mean, two minutes ago."

"Yeah, that's it," Daryl said. "Doris and I just met two minutes ago!"

"And you're already calling her Doris?" Marian questioned.

"I mean, Mrs. Benson," Daryl said. "Well, I, you know, she kind of looks like a Doris."

"I apologize for how awkward this is," Doris said. "I tried to call you, Marian, but you didn't answer. The power is out at my place and I needed a place to stay."

"I left my cell phone in the car. Sorry, mom."

"It's not a problem," Doris said, "it's just that ..." She hesitated, waving her hand in Daryl's direction. "I was caught off guard by seeing him here."

"Well, looks like it's time for girl's night out," Daryl said. "I need to be going!"

"No," Marian said.

"Really, it's been fun but it's getting kind of late," Daryl said.

"Daryl, I don't see why you have to leave just because ..." Marian stopped in mid-sentence. "Wait! Mother! Him?"

"Yup," Doris said.

"Are you serious?" Marian said.

Daryl grinned nervously at the two women. He needed to get out of there and quick. Without saying goodbye, he rushed out the front door.

Daryl mumbled to himself as he walked out of the house. "Great. I meet the potential love of my life and find out I've been sleeping with my future mother-in-law. All in one night!"

As he headed down the driveway he saw a man walking toward the house. Daryl didn't recognize the figure at first, but there was no mistaking him as the two men came closer.

"Dad?"

"Daryl? What are you doing here?"

Daryl shook his head and continued walking to his car.

Zelda's Friends

"Age is strictly a case of mind over matter. If you don't mind, it doesn't matter."

Jack Benny

"He's not wearing any pants!" Sheila exclaimed.

Zelda Rosenberg ignored her daughter.

Shelia's eyes widened. "Mother, he's not wearing any pants! Or underwear, either!"

Charles Fielding continued past the two women, naked from the waist down and unconcerned with the protests. His pasty body wriggled as he ran.

"So, you have a problem with a man having a little fun? You know, just because you're old doesn't mean you can't go crazy every now and then," Zelda said as they reached her room in the assisted living facility.

"Sure, he can have fun, but he was naked."

"Naked, smekid!" Zelda said. "I've seen a few tally whackers in my day."

"What?"

The conversation caught the attention of Zelda's roommate, Jacquelyn Blouth. "Is there something I should know about?" Jacquelyn was a tiny woman who wore thick eyeglasses too big for her face. Her white curly hair looked like a clown wig.

"Oh nothing," Zelda promised. "Just Charles taking his afternoon walk naked. And it wasn't that bad. Today, only the lower half of his body was showing."

"Such a nice man," Jacqueline said. "And not suffering from dementia like so many of the men here."

Shelia shook her head. She stared at her mother. Zelda was always a small woman with a thick frame, but Shelia noticed how her posture had changed. She slouched more, as if she was shrinking. Her hair seemed grayer and thinner, and her hands weak and frail. Her once vibrant blue eyes were lighter and glossed over.

Shelia had heard nothing but good things about the Abandonmaandpa Retirement Center. It was rated as one of the best on the south side of Eugene. The place was clean, and the employees seemed dedicated when Shelia had applied and subsequently admitted her mother.

This was Shelia's first visit since placing her mother in the home six months earlier.

"So, this is your first visit in six months? Time flies. Does this mean I'll be seeing you more often?" Zelda asked.

"Maybe, mother. But you have to remember that things have been crazy since Bob was transferred to Portland, and you are kind of far away."

"You can be here in less than two hours," Zelda said.

"You two need privacy?" Jacqueline asked.

"No, no. Shelia and I have nothing to keep from you. Everyone knows my son-in-law is an alcoholic and my granddaughter sleeps around."

"Mother!"

"What? You put me here so I couldn't spill the beans about the family in Portland, but you can't keep me from talking in here." Zelda pinched her lips and clenched her fists.

Jacqueline stood and smiled. "I think I will go visit the common area for awhile."

Zelda and Shelia watched in silence as Jacqueline left the room.

"Now that one, that one you really have to watch out for," Zelda said.

Shelia hesitated before responding. "She walks around naked, also?"

"Oh, worse. Far worse."

"What could be worse?"

"She pops biscuits all night long," Zelda said, waving her hands in the air. "And the odor could wake the dead!"

"Pops biscuits?"

"Air biscuits! Farts! She lets 'em rip," Zelda said. "If I don't fall asleep before she does, I'm treated to a symphony of her farting, and I panic that I'm gonna be gassed to death. And then sometimes, her snoring is so loud it wakes me, and it smells like I'm in some kind of gaseous swamp!"

"Have you talked to anyone about getting a new roommate?"

"Why the hell would I want to do that?" Zelda snapped. "She's my best friend in here and one of the nicest people I've ever met."

"So, mom, I've missed you," Shelia said, changing the subject. She really did miss her mother and the guilt of putting her in this place haunted her at night.

"Uh-huh."

"Do you like it here?"

"It's all right. It's not as nice as the home I had. The one you kicked me out of. You remember, don't you?"

"Now, momma, you know we've had this conversation before," Shelia said. "We both know you were getting too old to care for yourself. There was just no room for you in the house, especially with Bob and the kids. Besides, you would have to make new friends if you had moved with us."

"I had to make new friends here. And your brother, Wally, didn't have room for me, either. He's not even married."

"Momma," Shelia interrupted. "Momma, you know you wouldn't fit in with Wally and his friends. They're, they're…"

"Gay. I know he's gay. I've always known," she said. "I knew Wally was gay when he was twelve. When his male cousins visited, they wanted to play football outside and all he wanted to do was critique the dresses the actresses were wearing at the Academy Awards."

The two women laughed. The comment seemed to break the tension.

"Well," Shelia said, shaking her hands erratically, "some of the dresses were stunning!"

"Yes, they were."

"So, I'll ask again. Do you like it here? What are the people like? I saw the naked guy and you told me about your flatulent roommate. What are the rest of these folks like?"

"Good people, really good people," Zelda said. "Take Mr. Landis down the hallway. One of the nicest men I've ever known. Just one quirk, though."

"What's that?"

"Thinks he's Richard Nixon. Never in my life have I known anyone who thought they were Nixon. Elvis, yes. McArthur, I can see. Even Lincoln, but never Nixon!"

"It's that bad?"

"If he gets in your way, he yells, 'pardon me, pardon me!' Once I misplaced my room key and he ran down the hallway. You know what he said?"

"No."

"He tells me, 'you may think I took your key. Well I did not take your key, because I am not a crook!'"

155

Zelda chuckled to herself. Her daughter had a lot of nerve putting her in here, but at least it was entertaining.

Zelda continued. "Miss Timmons is sweet on Mr. Landis. She's never been married. Her nieces and nephews put her in here. But she knows that he's the one. Many a times, she's snuggled close to him during group activities and told him that she would be his campaign manager anytime."

"Why would she want to be with a kook like him?"

"A kook like him? Let me tell you, she ain't exactly playing with a full deck either."

Zelda looked out her window. The staff allowed them onto the grounds periodically, but only for brief intervals. There was no life beyond the grounds of the home. At least not for the residents.

"Let's go down the hall," Zelda said. "I want to see what Jacqueline and the others are doing. I'm lonely."

"We just got to your room. Besides, how can you be lonely? I'm here."

"I'm going down that hall. You want to join me, you can."

"Okay, mother. I just thought that since …"

Zelda stood and walked toward the door before her daughter could finish. Shelia followed, hurt by her mother's behavior. She didn't want to put her mother in here but she had no choice. She fought with Bob numerous times over whether her mother could live with them, but it was always a flat-out "no." And Wally was too busy with his own life to get involved.

The hallway leading to the common area was dingy. Shelia realized that she had only seen parts of the retirement center when she had her mother admitted. The walls looked like they hadn't been painted in years, and the only color in the room were the cardboard decorations staff members had tacked to the gray walls. For the residents, though, there was solace to be found on the bulletin boards with announcements of the different church and community groups scheduled to visit. At least for the residents who could still read the announcements.

"And there they are," Zelda said as she and Shelia approached the entrance to the common area. Jacqueline, Mr. Landis, and Miss Timmons were huddled around a table. The conversation was animated.

"Now Kennedy, Kennedy was ruthless. I could have beat him in 1960 if I had campaigned harder," Mr. Landis said. He was tall and lanky, and his corduroy pants were hiked up over his bellybutton. Miss Timmons looked on at him adoringly.

"Kennedy my foot!" Jacqueline yelled. "You never once as much saw Kennedy or Nixon for that matter."

"Never saw Nixon? I AM Nixon," Landis said.

"Phooey!"

"And I suppose you think you're someone important," Miss Timmons said.

"Well, my name is Jacqueline. If Mr. Landis knew John Kennedy, I'm sure he knows who I am."

Landis was taken aback by the claim. "You are her," he said pointing at Jacqueline. "You Kennedy woman, you!"

"Are they serious?" Shelia was concerned with the company her mother kept.

"Are they serious? They don't even know if they're serious," Zelda said as they got closer to the table. "So, can we join you?"

"Of course, please do," Mr. Landis said, standing to greet the women. "And who is this young lady with you, Zelda?"

"This is my daughter, Shelia," Zelda said as the two sat down.

"My pleasure," Mr. Landis said. "I'm Ron Landis."

"Ron Landis! I thought you were Richard Nixon," Jacqueline said.

Mr. Landis shot Jacqueline as disapproving look. "She knows who I *really* am. I just have to be humble about the situation."

"Of course, Mr. President," Shelia said.

Zelda leaned in toward her daughter and whispered, "Please don't feed the animals."

"Has anyone heard anything more about Mr. Winstone?" Miss Timmons asked.

"No, not since this morning," Jacqueline said. "I'm sure he's fine. You know how he loves to be dramatic."

Shelia was intrigued by the conversation. "Mr. Winstone?"

"He had heart pains this morning and an attendant *finally* took him away. But the attendant should be fine," Zelda said.

"Why would you be concerned with the attendant if Mr. Winstone was the one having heart pains?"

Mr. Landis interrupted the exchange between Zelda and her daughter, waving his right hand erratically as he spoke. "Because you don't know Harold! He does this crap all the time. He starts whining this morning that his chest is hurting, so an attendant is called."

"The attendant wants to take him down the hall to the infirmary," Jacqueline said, continuing the story. "But Harold wants to finish eating his Cheerios. But the attendant said he had to see a doctor immediately, so he tries to pull Harold away from the table."

"So what happens next?" Shelia asked.

"Harold does what any self respecting man would do when someone comes between him and his Cheerios," Mr. Landis said. "He punches the attendant in the groin and finishes his Cheerios. Another attendant is called who escorts him to his room for the remainder of the day, while the first attendant wails on the floor in a fetal position."

"Harold didn't have heart pains in the first place," Miss Timmons said. "So what's there to worry about?"

Shelia sniffed at a pungent odor that suddenly filled the air. "Goodness! What is that smell? Is that your dinner?"

Zelda frowned and nodded toward Jacqueline, who was blissfully unaware of her small contribution to the air around them.

"Attention residents." Shelia was taken back by the loud, muffled voice blaring from a speaker in a corner of the room. "It is five o'clock and dinner is now being served in the main dining hall. Please begin making your way to the area immediately."

Zelda's friends immediately stood and began walking away from the table.

"Oh goody, dinner," Mr. Landis said looking at Shelia. "Will you be joining us?"

"Well, I suppose I could," Shelia said.

"No, she's got to get back home," Zelda said.

Mr. Landis looked at Shelia despondently. "That's a pity."

The three continued walking toward the dining hall.

"That's a pity. Oh goody, dinner," Zelda said, mocking Mr. Landis. "Every night it's either cold roast beef, watery spaghetti, or dried chicken. And the dessert is either rubbery gelatin or a pudding that has no flavor. And yet he gets excited."

Shelia sighed. "You know, we could always reexamine the situation if you're not happy here."

"You mean come live with you and the rest of the family in Portland?"

"You know that wouldn't work. I was thinking, though, that maybe we could look at another assisted living facility. It's just that the people around here seem so …" Shelia's voice trailed off.

"Odd? Perverted? Juvenile?"

"Well, yes."

"Oh, they are and you didn't meet or hear about some of the odder ones. And I'm sure that most of them would have stories about me for their relatives that are real doozies!"

"So why put up with them?"

"They're my best friends now. They're the most important people in my life, even with their flatulence, illusions of grandeur, and attacks on the staff. They're all I've got left."

Shelia was taken aback. She felt a little sick. How could her mother say that? "You've still got me. And Nick is not that far away. I bet your friends don't even know you have a grandson at Pacific University."

"Of course they don't. You think he writes or takes time to come visit his grandmother?"

The two women were silent.

"You go now," Zelda said. "I'm hungry and I know you have to get back home to see friends."

"Mother, you know I love you. It's just that…"

"I love you, too. But you've got your friends and I've got mine now."

"You know, I'll be back at Christmas, right? Maybe this time, Bob and the kids can join me."

"Maybe. You never know. I may be running Landis' campaign by then and might be busy."

Zelda stood and made her way to the dining hall, turning to share one final thought with her daughter. "Don't worry about me, Shelia. Whether I like it or not, I'm home."

The Other Side Of Dexter Lake

"Perhaps they are not stars, but rather openings in heaven where the love of our lost ones pours through and shines down upon us to let us know they are happy."

Eskimo Proverb

The early morning light illuminated the darkened kitchen of the young man's home. The sunshine brightened the room just enough so he didn't need to turn on the overhead light as he sat at the table and began writing. He was young, and his eyes had yet to be ravaged like the rest of his body.

He took a pen from the table and began writing her the letter. There was not much time before he had to pick her up. Writing did not come easy for him, but this correspondence would be easy. He knew what he wanted to tell her, and creating the letter only demanded that he transferred words from his mouth and heart to the paper.

One day, what you think of now as pain will seem no more than a journey. What you know today as hurt will eventually lead to smiles, although they may be bittersweet. But you will come to know this experience as one laced with triumphs, because the highs will come with lows. Then you will come to see it all as part of a journey.

And one day, though it may be many years or even decades from now, you will cross Dexter Lake. And when you do, you come to a home. You have not seen it before, because it was not there when you looked out on the water. You will arrive there in an instant, almost as if you were transported there like wind traveling rapidly upon the lake. You will enter cautiously, but it will be designed with decorations that seem familiar to you, fragrances you have smelled before. There will be the sounds of laughter, all of it creating a sense of remembrance in your mind.

Other rooms will bring memories of harder times, followed by several hallways, each of which will lead to rooms that are even brighter, happier, and more exciting than the first ones you encountered. And finally, you will come to a large room. It will be empty, silent, and you will feel alone. And through a door on the other side of that room, someone will emerge. You will not recognize him at first, but he will know who you are, for he will have been waiting for you. And then he will smile at you. You will have never forgotten him, but will be taken aback at seeing him again. You will realize that you have finally found me again on the other side.

And then we will begin a feast and laugh and be filled with enthusiasm. And you will cry but this time, the tears will be tears of joy as we celebrate our reunion. And the meal we share will seem as if it will never end.

And it never will.

Josh glanced at what he had written before neatly folding it and placing it inside an envelope. He sealed the envelope and paused before writing on the front side. And then, like the contents of the letter inside, the words he wrote next came naturally:

"To my beloved Jennifer. Read three months from today."

Josh didn't know how much longer there was, but he was certain that three months was long enough. It was a certainty that by then, she would need the words he had chosen to share. He placed the note in his jacket, making sure he zipped the inside pocket to assure it would be safe until he found time to discreetly slip it into her purse when she was not looking.

The day looked as if it might be pleasant, but the approaching clouds bore witness to the weatherman's predictions that there would be storms later in the morning.

"Guess Weatherman Bob called it right after all," Josh said to himself.

He knew that forecasts of bad news by professionals seldom resulted in good tidings opposite of what they called for, regardless of whether it involved interpretation by a weatherman or a physician.

He dreamed that they were wrong about him, a hope that offered a figurative glimpse of sunlight much like the rays streaming into his house. But sunshine never lasted forever, and reality told him that while the light was real, the hope he longed for was probably not realistic.

Nor, as with the fleeting sunshine and the warmth that accompanied it, something he could see or feel.

***

The breeze from the approaching storm sent waves scampering across the lake and brought a chill to the fall air. The accompanying thunder and the darkening skies made the setting even more menacing. Jennifer snuggled closer to Josh, both for warmth and to express what she was feeling.

He had been to the lake dozens of times since his youth. Camping and fishing there as a boy, first with his parents and then with the Boy

Scouts, had led to water skiing trips during high school. He continued to return there even as he grew older, with trips in high school and then college, often accompanied by late night keg parties with his friends. He had kissed his first girlfriend there. The lake was part of who he was.

Jennifer had never been there until her first month in Oregon. She remembered the serenity of the area with its beautiful water, landscapes, and the boy, Josh, her friends had introduced her to. They met there and would always associate the lake with each other. The skies grew darker. The backdrop was not what they'd hoped for, but the clouds hung like a curtain ready to fall on the conclusion of their story.

Josh stared out on the water as the couple sat on a large rock near the lake's shore. "What secrets must be here. Dexter Lake can be both a paradise and a frightening destination at times," he said.

"It's getting kind of rough," Jennifer replied.

Josh snickered. "Does it matter, for me?" The days would be cold soon, and he knew there would be few times the weather would be nice.

Jennifer began crying.

"I'm sorry," he said. "Hey look!" Josh pointed out on the water as several fish jumped out of the water, most likely in an effort to increase their speed as they raced to a calmer section of the lake.

"You remember the first time we came here? It was a lot nicer that day," Jennifer said.

"Yeah, we met here. It was our freshmen year at the University of Oregon."

They had shared the story dozens of times, but they never tired of reliving the memories. He was a cocky fraternity pledge. She was a shy psychology major, unsure of why her girlfriends in the dormitory had invited her to a fraternity lake party. Her friends insisted that they had found the perfect boy for her, but she had her doubts.

"Did you know that you loved me the first time you saw me?" Jennifer asked.

"Of course I did," Josh said. "More than you know. When did you know the moment you loved me?"

"I guess the minute I looked at you."

"But you weren't ready to admit it, right?"

Jennifer hesitated before responding. She didn't want to hurt him. She never would and especially not now. "It's just that you were so …"

Her hesitation led him to complete her thought. "Cocky?"

"I guess."

"I was. I needed to be humbled. And outside of my parents, I never knew anyone I would come to love as much as you. I'm glad I met you."

"I am too," Jennifer said.

"My whole world changed the day I met you. I was reckless and immature then and never thought it would take a shy, quiet girl from Oatfield to tame me." Josh felt the strong gust of wind; it chilled him. He noticed that Jennifer was shaking. "It's getting cooler. We can go back to the car if you want."

"No, I want to stay here a few more minutes. It's nice with you here."

"Cold weather, dark skies, thunder, and all." Josh said. Jennifer chuckled at his sarcasm.

Josh looked onto the water. There was a sense of guilt that embarrassed him. He wouldn't leave her if he had a choice and she knew that. But he was abandoning her and, willingly or not, knew that men never leave. He hurt for her and he hurt for himself, pained by the reality of the future that they would not know together.

"You know, one day, you may meet another guy that reminds you of me. Maybe he'll be as good looking as me, and funny. And hopefully he won't be as cocky as I was the first time we met. Take time to listen to him, get to know him, and just maybe …"

"But he still won't be you." Jennifer choked back her tears.

Josh sighed. "Just as this lake looks menacing, we've been here when it's beautiful. We've seen the sun and the blue sky, we've gotten up early to watch the sun rise and said goodbye as it set. There's always lots of light before the darkness and the darkness always leads to light again. One day, you'll know beautiful light again. Both in the world and your life."

"And what about your life?"

"Jennifer, I've had you for five years. What could be more beautiful?"

"But now you can't be with me any longer. It's not fair. Why do you have to leave me?"

"But it's natural. Today you are hurt and soon you will feel intense pain," Josh said. "But it's only because of the joy that you — that we — have had together. Dexter Lake is dark and brooding today, but beauty will return to it. And there will be beauty again in your life. And happiness."

She couldn't wait longer for the question. She didn't want to ask, but she knew he had seen his physician the day before. "What is the latest?"

He didn't want to tell her the truth. "I still have cancer," Josh said. That much was true, but he didn't want her to know that the invader ravaging his body had progressed, and it was a certainty now that he would be gone in less than three months.

Jennifer looked away before glancing back at him. A small bittersweet smile brightened her tear-streaked face.

"It's time to head back," Josh said. He gazed out on the water, almost as if he saw where they would be reunited. "Jennifer, remember when I said I would never lie to you?"

"Yes."

"And I have always told you the truth? Right?"

"Of course."

Josh turned to face his fiancée before softly wrapping his arms around her waist.

"Then know this too is true — you *will* see me on the other side."

A Night at Walker Field

"I have never killed a man, but I have read many obituaries with great pleasure."

Clarence Darrow

Jason Spencer checked his watch for the third time in ten minutes. Willie was twenty minutes late and Jason was already sucking down his second beer. He was anxious because Willie knew what he was planning and it could really ruin his life if things went bad.

In the 20 years of marriage, Jason had never done anything wrong except for one affair. But, he had been successful in paying off "the other woman" when she threatened to tell his wife about the liaison, thus saving heartache for his wife and kids. Twenty thousand dollars to pay off a mistress was a lot, but Jason reasoned that it spoke volumes about his character that he was willing to give up that much money to avoid her hurting his family.

That was the beginning of his money problems. Jason couldn't believe he was one of the most respected professionals in his field and yet so far in debt. Paying off a mistress, gambling and strip clubs — not to mention living well past his family's means — had really put a dent on the family's budget.

But murdering his wife would result in a payoff by her life insurance and put him back on easy street, not to mention, sparing his two children the pain and humiliation of knowing their father had filed for bankruptcy.

His introspection was interrupted by the sound of rain when the front door of the small bar near Lake Oswego swung open and Willie stepped inside. Jason motioned for his friend to join him at a small table.

"You're late!" Jason said.

"In case you haven't noticed, it's kind of nasty out there," Willie said.

"Sit down and shut up."

"Geez," Willie replied as he sat down. "You're awfully grumpy tonight. What's the big emergency?"

"I've decided to do it and you're going to help me."

"Do what?"

"Kill Delores. I've had it with that bitch and getting rid of her will not only ensure not worrying about her anymore, it'll also guarantee that I can finally get out of debt once her life insurance pays off."

"Geez, you didn't call me out here just to start that crap again?" It wasn't the first time Jason had approached the subject, but each time

Willie had succeeded in convincing his friend of the foolishness of his plans.

"I'm serious, I've got to start planning this before she does something unfair like divorcing me and demanding that I pay her alimony!"

"Right," Willie said, "but you won't get a dime if the police find out you murdered her, only a lifetime stay in prison. And if you think that things aren't good now, just wait until 'fresh meat' becomes synonymous with your name." The two men were silent for a few seconds before Willie decided to humor his friend. "So, how do you want to do it? Shooting, stabbing?"

"Nah, neither one of those would work."

"Why, too messy?"

"It's not the clean up I'm worried about."

"Then what?"

Jason hesitated, reluctant to tell his friend the truth. "I'm squeamish. I can't stand the sight of blood."

"You can't stand the sight of blood?"

"And what if her brains splatter when we shoot her, or a limb, or organ is exposed? That would be too hard on me. I swear, I would lose it right there."

"Are you *sure* that divorce wouldn't be better?"

"Divorce does nothing to help the situation. Even if we divorce, I've still got the debt. Plus, I'd have to pay alimony and child support." Jason shook his head before taking another sip of his beer. "Besides, if I divorce her, she might fall in love with someone else. I wouldn't want to fuck up my kids' lives by saddling them with some asshole their mom hooks up with."

"You're right, murder would probably be easier on them."

"Of course it would. And I can always take them to Disneyland if there's any money left from her life insurance policy after I pay off my debt."

Willie could care less if he helped murder Delores. A conviction for shoplifting as a youth, and a conviction as an adult for receiving stolen property meant he wasn't afraid to break the law — as long as he didn't get caught again. He just wanted to do the right thing for his friend.

"Okay, first we gotta think about the body once she's dead," Willie said. "That's the most important thing to make sure we don't get caught.

Let's think about where we should put her body, then we can talk about killing her later."

"You mean, kind of like planning a funeral for a loved who's dying, only this would be to keep ourselves out of jail?"

"Exactly!"

"You got any ideas?"

"I don't know," Willie said. "Walker Field is not too far away. You know, there's nothing but trees and open areas there. As big as it is, surely we could find a place there to bury her. When do you want to do this?"

"Last week."

"Okay, then. Let's go out there now and scout out a location."

"In case you haven't noticed, it's raining."

"In case you haven't noticed, it always rains in Portland. That's why it's the perfect time to do this," Willie reasoned. "This way, we'll know how soft the soil gets. Think of this as a field test for the burial."

"Oh yeah, but what do I tell her if she sees the mud on my shoes?"

"You said last week that you two are always arguing, so tell her it's none of her goddamn business."

"Yeah, but the reason we're going to the field is because of her."

"But she doesn't have to know that, at least not until we bury her there."

"We can't screw this up."

"Don't worry, I'm too smart for that," Willie said. "Trust me, I'm not going to let a little mud on your shoes derail your plans."

Jason took another swig from his beer and laid a ten dollar bill on the table. "Okay, let's do it. I gotta piss first, though."

"Piss when we get there. Think of it as christening her grave before she's even buried."

***

The Chief of the 4th precinct never liked the idea. Having a husband and wife team travel as police officers never seemed like a good plan. But Harry and Mildred were good cops and it was what they wanted. It didn't violate any policies, and letting them work together helped keep them from being bored as they hashed out family problems in the cop car.

The two had just turned onto the main road when they saw two men siding off to the side near Walker Field.

"Want to stop and take a look?" Mildred asked.

"Yeah, I think that might be a good idea," Harry said as he placed the car in park and turned on its flashing lights.

Jason hadn't noticed the vehicle approaching and was startled when he saw the flashing lights. "Oh crap, what are the cops doing here?"

"Chill. Just tell them we're here to have sex," Willie said.

"What?"

"Yeah, a lot of gays come in here to get it on. You didn't know that?"

"You wanna bury my wife in a field where fags hang out? What's wrong with you?"

"Oh, the queers won't care."

"Good evening, gentlemen," Harry said as he approached the men and shined a light in their faces. Mildred stepped out, but stayed near the car. "You two mind telling me exactly what you're doing out here alone on a rainy night?"

"Just talking," Jason said.

"Just talking?" Harry asked.

"Yeah," Willie said. "We're not doing anything immoral if that's what you think."

"So you must be here for some other reason, then," Harry said. "Right?"

"Actually, no," Willie said.

"Then you are here for sex?" Harry asked.

"No! I mean, yes," Willie said.

Harry grinned. He wasn't sure what they were planning, but he had a sense that they would be easy to wear down. Turning, he motioned for Mildred to join him. "You take the one in the suit and I'm going to take this guy in the jeans," he said. "I don't know what they're doing here, but I'm sure it's bad news."

Harry motioned to Jason. "Listen, this pretty woman here wants to have a word with you while I talk to your buddy. Okay?"

"Sure," Jason said.

Harry walked a few feet to where Willie was standing. He looked like a derelict. His hair was uncombed, his shirt was missing three buttons, the knees of his pants dirty. "You doing all right tonight?'

"Wonderful," Willie said.

"Now, I bet if I ask nicely, I can get you to tell me what y'all are doing here right now."

"Nothing, honest."

"Just two men alone in a field at night when it's raining? You don't think that sounds a little suspicious?" Harry could tell Willie was starting to sweat.

"Listen, I don't want to mess things up for my buddy. He's a surgeon, you know, and he can't afford to have anything bad come out about him."

"Look, if you guys were out here for a little close order drill, I'll understand."

"Oh hell no, we're not gay. Hell no," Willie said. "Okay, we were here for a reason, but it's nothing that bad."

"Then why are you here?"

Willie hesitated, suddenly nervous again and unable to think of a lie that would keep them out of trouble.

"Look, I really don't care why you're here," Harry said, "but don't insult my intelligence by telling me that two men were standing in a field known for immoral activity and they weren't up to anything. Especially when it's raining."

"You really don't care why we're here?"

"Makes no difference to me."

"So if I tell you that we were here for homosexual activity you really won't care?"

"Not at all."

"And you won't arrest us?"

"I didn't say that."

"Yeah, but if you arrest us, they'll put our names in the paper and people will think we're gay."

"That's probably true."

"No, it's not true. It's not true," Willie said. "Because I ain't no fag."

"Then tell me what you're doing here."

"Okay, okay. I'll tell the truth if it'll keep me from being identified in the newspaper as a homosexual. We were going to kill her. That's all!"

"What?"

"We were going to kill Jason's wife. We were looking for a place to bury her after we did it, but we weren't here for sex. Okay?"

Harry sighed, both in frustration and to suppress laughter before reaching for the handcuffs attached to his belt. Spinning Willie around, he quickly snatched the man's arms behind him and slapped on the handcuffs.

"Hey, what the hell are you doing?" Willie asked.

"I'm placing you under arrest."

"Why?"

"Because you were so worried about being labeled as a homosexual that you just confessed that you were out here planning to bury your friend's wife after you killed her," Harry said. "And that means you're both going to be charged with conspiracy to commit murder, you moron."

Mildred looked up to see Willie being cuffed and Harry motioned for her to do likewise with Jason.

"Mildred, have I got a story for you when we get home," Harry said. "I want you to remember this dumbass the next time you start talking about how your cousin Shirley can't keep her mouth shut."

***

Phil rolled his eyes. She was blabbing from the other room. She always went on about how bad her day had been. He should just kill her and get it over with. Blah blah blah. He hoped she would just shut up, for the love of God, and come to bed.

"I swear, sometimes I think I'm the only one at the club that has a lick of sense. And then the waiter at the restaurant. I swear he has the IQ of a house plant. You would think that …"

"Holy shit!" Phil yelled.

"What? What?" She ran into the bedroom; her face was splattered with moisturizing cream.

"Listen! Listen!" he said, pointing at the evening news on the television.

"Apparently," the television anchor said, "two men were arrested while scouting out a location to bury the wife of one of the men after they murdered her. The two men have been identified as Jason Spencer and his friend Willie Parsons."

The couple looked at each other in disbelief. "I hope you are finished talking about what a bad day you had," Phil said, "because you know what this means, don't you?"

"Things are definitely looking better."

"Not only do we not have to worry about Jason having a legal reason to divorce you if he ever finds out about us, now we don't have to worry about knocking him off," Phil said. "See, you didn't have such a bad day after all, did you?"

She grinned before dropping the towel she was wearing and joining him in bed.

"Good night, Phil."

Phil turned off the television with the remote, followed by switching off a small lamp on a table next to the bed.

"Good night, Delores."

Poetry in Disarray

"There's nothing wrong with revenge. It's the best way to get even!"
Archie Bunker

Stepping from the shower into the locker room alone,
he hears a noise, looks around, and picks up the buzzing phone.
He flips it open, checks the number, and holds it to his ear,
"Hey, handsome," comes the whisper, low but clear.
"I had to call," the voice continued, "and last night was the best,
I've never seen such stamina, you're better than the rest.
I've had men, too many men, but darling, when you did that little thing,
you know the one, t'was with your tongue, you really made me sing!
You are GOD in bed. Why, I can scarce stand up today!
What a loon your wife must be, to let you slip away!"

He starts to ask the question, but she says, "Oh, do you think,
that I could go out shopping? See, I found the perfect mink,
to wear with that black dress — you know, the one that's cut so low?
You nearly tore it off me Sunday evening, don't you know!
I need some shoes as well, I saw a darling little pair.
I thought I'd use your charge card, I don't suppose you care?"
He hesitates, she laughs and waits, he feels a reckless urge,
"All right," he grins, she laughs again, he feels his hormones surge.
"Why not?" he says, and leans his back against the locker door,
encouraged by permission granted, now she asks for more.

"My dear," she purrs, "While I've got you on the phone right here
I'd better put a bug about next Sunday in your ear.
Don't tell me you've forgotten? Why, surely you must know!
It's our anniversary, we met one year ago!
You promised me a necklace, with a black Tahitian pearl,
I know it costs a hundred grand, but you know that I'm your girl!
I've found the one I want, but, hon, we've got no time to lose,
that Celia Blass from yoga class said that's the one she'd choose!"
He gets the picture, smiles and murmurs, "Dear...what can I say?
Just pick it up and charge it, you can have your gift today."

She laughs again, and just the sound sends shivers up his spine,
He thinks, "This day is really turning out just fine!"
As if on cue, she whispers, "Can you guess what I am wearing?
Oh, wait, you're out in public, right? I'll stop the over-sharing.
I wouldn't want to make you, well, indecent, now, you know?
Why that could be embarrassing, to give the world a show!"
He calms her fear: "I promise, dear, I'm very much alone,
so if you rouse my trouser mouse, it's you, me, and the phone!"
She laughs in sheer delight at this and brazenly reveals
she's clad in just a scarlet negligee and matching heels.

She giggles, and he feels the thrill that only she can bring,
"Oh dear, it nearly slipped my mind, the most important thing!
The shop just called — that pole I hit last Tuesday at the mall?
It bent the frame and crushed the trunk, and that's not even all.
The Jag's a total loss, they said, there's too much damage done,
but it's all right, I called and had a chat with Mr. Bunn.
A short trip to his dealership, and I found just the ride,
it's meant for me, you'll have to see! Red leather all inside!
It has a funny name, I think he called it a 'Pagani,'
Italian, right? And you'd look great in it in your Armani."

He tells her, "Charge it!" and he feels his senses spin,
he swears that just listening to her has to be a sin.
She says, "Come over late tonight, I've got some wine to share,
and underneath this red silk slip I have no underwear!"
She hangs up, and behind him he can hear an opening door,
a man strides in and glares around, he's seen the chap before.
The guy is rude; his attitude makes him a piece of work,
he is an ass and thinks his cash means he can be a jerk.
"Where's my phone!!" the man snaps, our hero smiles and turns to say,
"This must be yours I found. Oh, and have a lovely day!"